www.thebeautifulgamebooks.co.uk

ORCHARD BOOKS
338 Euston Road, London NW1 3BH
Orchard Books Australia
Level 17/207 Kent Street, Sydney, NSW 2000

First published in 2011 by Orchard Books

A Paperback Original

ISBN 978 1 40830 426 6

Text © Narinder Dhami 2011

A CIP catalogue record for this book is available
from the British Library.

1 3 5 7 9 10 8 6 4 2

Printed in the UK

Orchard Books is a division of Hachette Children's Books,
an Hachette UK company.

www.hachette.co.uk

THE BEAUTIFUL GAME

Friends and football – the perfect match

KATY'S REAL LIFE

NARINDER DHAMI

ORCHARD BOOKS

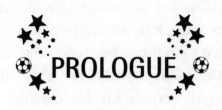

PROLOGUE

Katy ran down the street, her heart thumping with panic. She could see the bus in the distance and she still had to get to the bus stop. Would she make it? *She had to. She could not miss this bus.*

To Katy's relief, there were a couple of people at the stop. As they climbed onto the bus, she joined the back of the queue and waited her turn to get on and pay. She had the coins clutched in her hand, but she was so flustered, she dropped them on the floor of the bus and they rolled everywhere.

'Sorry!' Katy gasped to the driver, who was looking quite annoyed. Quickly she collected them up, paid her fare and scuttled off to an empty seat at the back.

As the bus moved off, Katy leaned her burning forehead on the cold glass of the window. She took deep breaths, one after the other, trying to calm herself down. It was difficult, though, because the bus was taking her in the opposite direction, right away from where Katy *should* be going.

Katy didn't often cry, but right now she'd never felt so down and depressed in her whole life. Would the other girls forgive her for deserting them at such a hugely important moment? Would they understand that Katy simply had to put her family first this time?

Katy hoped desperately that they would. But she just couldn't be sure.

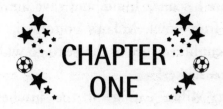

CHAPTER ONE

'Kay-teee! *KAY-TEE!*'

'Milan, be quiet!' I jumped off the window seat and tiptoed into the kitchen past my dad, who was asleep on the saggy old sofa. He hadn't been very well again yesterday, which made four nights in a row he hadn't been able to sleep. 'What's the matter *now*?'

My little brother Milan was in our shoe box sized kitchen (no, really, it IS the size of a shoe box). He beamed up at me. 'I'm hungry, Katy,' he announced.

'What, again?' I said sternly. 'You've had two biscuits already.' The problem is, it's just *sooo* difficult to be stern with Milan because he's incredibly cute! He's only four years old and he has dark hair the same colour as mine, but his is curly and glossy instead of sleek and smooth. I'd kill for those curls! And he also has these huge chocolate-brown eyes that melt me every time. I'm such a sucker.

'No more biscuits,' I said, and gave him an apple from the fruit bowl. Milan's bottom lip wobbled a bit, so I cut him a slice of cheese to go with it. Told you I was a sucker!

Leaving Milan eating at the kitchen table, I hurried back to the front window. I was looking out for my mum, who'd gone to her early morning cleaning job. It was a grey, blowy March morning, but I didn't care because it was Saturday and that meant FOOTBALL. One of my favourite things in the whole world. I'd joined the Springhill Stars Under-Thirteens team almost exactly a year ago, and most Saturday mornings during the season I'd sat here worrying that my mum wouldn't get home from work in time for me to make it to the match. Today we were playing the Pickford Panthers. Mum was a bit later than usual, and I was getting anxious. We only had three games left until the end of the season, and the Stars were in the running for promotion to the next league. But to do that, we had to overtake our biggest rivals, the Blackbridge Belles, because only the top team went through automatically. The next four teams had to go into the play-offs. Scary!

Since we'd narrowed the gap between us and the Belles to one point, just before Christmas, things had been up and down. We'd got knocked out of the County Cup in the third round, and we'd lost a league game here and there. To our dismay, we'd dropped back to three points behind the Belles by the end of January. But then we'd pulled ourselves together a bit and the Belles had had a bad spell, which meant the gap was now back to one point again.

'Can I have some more cheese, Katy?' Milan called from the kitchen. I jumped up and went in to him again.

'No,' I whispered, putting my finger to my lips. 'And don't wake Dad up.'

It wasn't just Saturdays, either, when I had to be at home. My mum worked every day of the week except Sundays, and someone had to be around to watch Milan because my dad wasn't always well enough to do it. Mum worked so hard, she didn't always have time to do the shopping and cooking and cleaning, so I helped out with that, too. I had to juggle things like crazy – housework and homework and school and matches and training twice a week and seeing my friends. I was *always* clock-watching.

I know that Jasmin, Georgie, Grace, Hannah and Lauren think there's something mysterious about me. I was having a pretty stressful time a month or two ago when Dad was quite ill, and after training one day, I was outside the changing-room door while the others were inside. I heard Jasmin say 'Look, why don't we just *ask* her what's going on? It's totally obvious that something's not right, and we might be able to help.'

I guessed instantly that the girls were talking about me.

'You know what Katy's like,' Georgie had said. 'She doesn't tell us *anything* about her home life.'

'If we asked, I'd feel like we were sticking our noses in.' That was Lauren. 'We ought to wait until Katy tells us herself – *if* she wants to.'

I went into the changing-room then, and the girls stopped talking about me and started discussing the match that coming Saturday instead. I was relieved, but I also felt a bit upset that they *hadn't* questioned me about what was wrong. I didn't want them to, really, because I admit that I *do* get a bit prickly and embarrassed sometimes when I'm asked things I don't want to answer. But this time I sort of hoped they *would*. Do you understand that? Because I don't!

Anyway, whatever the girls think, there's nothing very mysterious about my real life...

Dad, Mum, Milan and me came to England from Poland just over three years ago. We used to live in a little village about fifty kilometres south of Warsaw (which is the capital city of Poland, if you didn't know!). My grandparents still live there, and we had to leave our little dog, Max, with them, which upset me a lot. My gran writes every week and tells us how Max is doing.

At first, everything in England was fine. We came to Melfield because some of my mum and dad's friends from Poland were already here, and my dad found work straightaway. He's a carpenter, and he made all our furniture back home. I could already speak English quite well because we were studying it at school. My dad speaks English brilliantly – he'd visited England a few times before and he likes watching English and American films. Dad often spoke English to me and Milan at home because he wanted us to be good at different languages. My mum didn't like that much because she only speaks Polish. Anyway, I'm glad Dad *did* help me improve my English because when we moved here, it didn't really take me long to fit in.

Lots of things are different here to Poland, though, and it took me *so* long to get used to them! Everyone thinks Poland is really cold in winter, and it is, but England feels so much colder. My dad says it's because it's so damp and wet here. In Poland the snow makes everything look really pretty, and people are ready for it, so everything goes on mostly as normal. Here in England, everything seems to stop for snow!

There are *so* many more people in England, too. I looked up *Warsaw* and *London* on the internet in the library, and Warsaw has about 1.7 million people while London has eight million. EIGHT MILLION – it's amazing, isn't it? My dad took us to London once on a sight-seeing trip before he got ill, and I think most of those eight million people were there in Trafalgar Square at the same time as us!

Most people in Poland don't have as much stuff as people in England do, either. That's another difference. There's so much choice here – clothes, shoes, food, drink, books, TV programmes and everything else – it makes my head spin. It doesn't really matter that much, though, because we don't have a lot of spare money to spend, anyway. Not since Dad became ill about six months after we arrived.

'The doctor told your dad that he has ME,' Mum had explained after Dad had had lots of tests at the local hospital. For the last few months he'd always been tired and run-down and he complained of aching all over and not being able to sleep.

'What's that?' I'd asked fearfully. I'd never heard of it before, and I was secretly very frightened that Dad was going to die. It wasn't as serious as that, although it was still very scary. But now his mysterious illness had a name at last – myalgic encephalomyelitis (I *think* I've got that right). So I was hoping the doctors would be able to help Dad get better.

But I was shocked to discover that there's no real cure for ME. The doctor said Dad had to learn to 'manage it and live with it'. I Googled ME at the library to find out more about it, and some people don't even believe that it's a real disease at all, which *totally* annoyed me! When Dad is in a bad way, he's *really* exhausted, not just 'tired' like you and me. He described it to me once as feeling like he'd never get out of bed again because his body wouldn't even be able to cope with standing up for a few minutes.

So then, as you can guess, everything changed completely. Dad couldn't work any more. Some days were better than others, but even when he was feeling brighter, he tired very quickly. He'd always loved visiting different places and meeting new people, but now he couldn't do any of those things. He hardly ever complained, though, because my dad's just not like that. On the days he was feeling better, he watched TV and listened to the radio, and read all the newspapers, Polish and English, and we borrowed books from the library for him.

In the end, though, Mum had to go out and get a job. She was really worried because she doesn't speak English very well, but she managed to find a cleaning job with a company run by a Polish couple. She cleans offices in different parts of town early in the mornings and then again in the evenings.

And what about me? Well, *someone* has to look after Milan while Mum's at work or out shopping, if Dad's feeling ill. I know it annoys the other girls sometimes that I can't always say straight away if I can go to someone's house on Sunday or whatever. That's because I always have to check with Mum first. She's great about letting me go out whenever I can, and she and Dad both love the fact that I play for the Stars. So far Mum's *never* let me down, and she's always made sure she gets home in time for me to make it to the matches on Saturdays.

I glanced at the clock again. Mum was *really* late now, later than she'd ever been before. I'd noticed that she seemed to be working longer and longer hours recently. I'd put my jacket on a few minutes ago so I'd be ready to leave the *second* she got back, and now I took my phone out of my jacket pocket and tried to ring her. I just got her voicemail, so I sent a text.

'Your mother isn't back yet, *kochanie?*' Dad had just opened his eyes and caught me staring anxiously out of the window. *Kochanie* is Polish for 'darling' or 'honey' or something like that in English, anyway!

'Not yet,' I replied, trying not to sound worried. Dad was heavy-eyed, his face was grey and colourless and he kept coughing, too. I hated seeing him like this. I could remember him back home in Poland when he was handsome and laughing and always busy in his workshop.

'You go, Katy,' Dad said, pulling himself upright on the sofa. He coughed a little. 'It's an important game, isn't it? I can look after Milan till your mama gets home.'

'No, it's OK—' I began.

'Just go!' Dad broke in, smiling at me. 'She'll be home in the next ten minutes or so. Even Milan can behave himself for ten minutes!'

'Want to bet?' I asked. 'But thanks, Tata. If you're sure.'

I gave him a huge hug and then dashed into the kitchen to see what Milan was up to because it had gone suspiciously quiet. I found him unwinding the roll of kitchen paper and wrapping it around his arms and legs.

'I'm playing hospitals,' Milan announced.

'Not any more.' I retrieved the kitchen paper and wound it back onto the roll as best as I could. 'Come on, I have to go, and you'll be a good boy for Tata, won't you?'

I tucked Milan onto the sofa next to Dad, grabbed my bag and went out, leaving them watching Saturday-morning cartoons on TV. Then I hurried downstairs, careful not to catch my foot in the hole in the carpet on the third step down. We rented the flat at the top of the house, and there were student nurses in the flat below us. We didn't really see them much, although we heard their parties sometimes!

I went out, closing the front door behind me. As I did so, I saw our new neighbour, Mrs Jackson, taking her milk inside. She'd recently bought the little house next door and had moved in just after Christmas.

'Hello,' I said politely across the low fence.

Mrs Jackson jumped and turned to peer suspiciously at me. Mumbling something that *might* have been *Hello*, she went inside and shut her door.

I shrugged. My parents had brought me up to be polite and respectful to elderly people, but Mrs Jackson was always the same – grumpy and grouchy! She kept herself to herself and didn't speak to anyone in our street. We only knew her name because the postman had accidentally put one of her letters through our letterbox.

As I ran for the bus, I wondered if Mrs Jackson didn't like us because we're Polish. Some English people don't. I've heard them make comments about us because we're foreign and my mum doesn't speak English. But I try not to let it upset me. Most people I meet are lovely, and my *best* mates – Grace, Georgie, Hannah, Grace and Lauren – are just the greatest mates ever! And I might never have met them at all if Mum and I hadn't gone into a charity shop in town that day, over a year ago...

'Do you like this, Katy?' Mum had taken a long pink skirt off the rail and was holding it against her. We bought a lot of our clothes in charity shops or in the sales. 'I think it might fit me.'

'It's nice, Mama.' I was flipping through the rack of girls' clothes near the counter, not really expecting to find anything, when something purple leapt out at me. It was a football shirt with *Springhill Stars* written across the front, and there was a pair of white shorts on the coat hanger with it.

'What's that?' Mum came over to see.

'It looks like a football kit,' I replied. 'But I don't recognise the team.'

We were speaking in Polish, but the man serving at the counter glanced at us and guessed what we were talking about.

'Are you interested in the football kit?' he asked.

'The Stars are a local girls' football club in the Springhill area of town.'

'Girls' football club!' I exclaimed, quickly translating that into Polish for Mum. I'd always loved football, watching it *and* playing it. By playing, I meant kicking a ball around with the kids in our village back home, not being part of a club.

'You'd love that, Katy,' Mum said. She hung the skirt she'd been going to buy back on the rail and picked the Stars kit up instead. 'Try it on and if it fits, let's buy it. Then you can go along to the club.'

'But, Mama!' I spluttered. 'We can't afford it, and anyway, we don't even know if the club *needs* any more players!'

'Then you'll have to fight for a place, won't you?' Mum said with a smile, handing me the kit. 'Go and try it on.'

The kit fitted me perfectly, I remembered with a smile as I sat down on the bus. It seemed like a good sign! Dad was all for me joining the Stars too, and he and Mum were thrilled when, after my very first training session, the coach, Freya Reynolds, put me straight into the team.

I'd been pleased to see Grace and Georgie there because they went to the same school as me, although I didn't really know them very well. A few weeks later Hannah joined the team, and I'd seen her around at school too. But the six of us, including Jasmin and Lauren, didn't become *really* good friends until Freya sent us on a football course during the Easter holidays last year. Now we're so close, we're almost like sisters.

Except that the others still don't know much about my 'real life'...

I sighed as I checked my watch. If I ran from the bus stop, I'd just make it to the college where we played our home matches before the game started.

I can guess what you're thinking. Yes, I *know* if I asked any of the other girls whether their parents would pick me up from home and drop me off after the game, they'd say yes straight away. But somehow, I just don't like to... I don't want to be a bother. No, I'll be honest, it's not only that. The real reason is that I'm a bit ashamed to let the girls see where we live. It's horrible feeling this way, but you'd understand if you saw our flat. It's quite shabby and small, and all the other girls live in houses that seem enormous compared to ours. Lauren's place is like a celebrity's mansion! So I don't really want them to visit, even though my mum and dad are always asking if they can meet them. Maybe someday.

Don't hate me for being this way, will you? I guess I'm just too proud, and a bit stubborn as well!

The bus stopped at the bottom of the road up to the college. I was already by the doors, waiting for them to open, and I leapt off and ran for it. Clutching my bag, I rushed through the car park, through the college and down the corridors to the changing-room at the back.

As I skidded around the last corner, I could see our coach, Ria, herding the Stars out of the changing-room. They all whooped with relief when they saw me running towards them.

'What time do you call this, Katy Novak?' Georgie yelled. 'Hurry up and get your backside out onto the pitch with the rest of us!'

'Am I the coach, Georgie, or are you?' Ria enquired. I *think* she was joking, but you never really know when Georgie and Ria get going! Ria replaced our old coach, Freya, at the start of this season, and she's been dating Georgie's dad for the last four months or so. Georgie's *kind* of OK with it now, but it was touch and go for a while whether she was actually going to stay in the team or not.

'*You're* the coach, Ria,' Georgie assured her breezily. 'I'm just the goalie with the big mouth.'

'How true,' Lauren remarked, her baby-blue eyes dancing with mischief.

'Shut it, you!' Georgie ordered, grabbing Lauren around the waist and sweeping her off her feet. Everyone grinned, including Ria, as Lauren kicked her legs helplessly and shrieked in protest. Lauren's so petite, she's like a pretty little doll. But she's a tiger on the pitch! She fights for every ball and she can run faster than any of us.

'I'll be out in two minutes,' I shouted as Ria led them outside. I could see through the glass doors that the Pickford Panthers were already on the pitch, and the ref was there too, chatting to the Panthers manager. I really *was* late. But at least I'd made it.

I stripped off in record time and jumped into my kit. Then I scooped everything up, including my bag, and shoved them all into one of the lockers.

As I ran for the door, I heard my phone go off inside my jacket. Someone was trying to call me. I hesitated, but only for a second. I really *didn't* have time to answer it.

It was probably just my mum apologising for being late home, I told myself as I headed out of the door. Nothing important.

I didn't find out until after the match just how wrong I was.

CHAPTER TWO

When I ran out onto the pitch, I was alarmed to see Grace, Georgie, Hannah and Lauren gathered around Jasmin, who was looking quite pale.

'What's the matter?' I asked.

'I feel sick!' Jasmin groaned, clutching her tummy. She'd scraped her shoulder-length black hair into two bouncy bunches tied with purple ribbons decorated with pink and green beads. Now I also noticed that she was wearing brand-new shiny gold football boots with bright pink laces. Jasmin likes to stand out wherever she goes! I love her to bits. She's *such* a sweetie. 'I don't think I can play—'

''Course you can.' Georgie slapped her on the back. 'It's probably just trapped wind!' We all giggled. 'You'll be OK once we get started.'

'I'm not feeling too great myself,' Hannah muttered, tucking her long chestnut hair behind her ears. There was a worried look in her green eyes. 'I'm just so *nervous*. I mean, we only have two more matches left to go after today. If we lose and the Belles win, we'll be *four* points behind them. And if we lose our next match and the Belles win, then they'll be *seven* points ahead of us and we won't be able to catch them.'

'Hannah's right,' Grace chimed in. 'We *have* to win today. I don't think I can face the play-offs.'

I glanced at her and was surprised to see that Grace didn't seem her usual laid-back and cheerful self. She's so gorgeous, she's like a model – tall and slim, blonde and blue-eyed. But today she looked a bit washed-out, as if she hadn't slept well last night. I wondered if it was because of her mum and dad. Mr and Mrs Kennedy had split up near the end of last year and Grace and her twin sister Gemma were waiting anxiously to find out if their parents were going to try again or just get divorced.

'We are NOT going into the play-offs!' Georgie

declared loudly, frowning at Grace. She jammed her baseball cap onto her head, stuffing her wild, curly, black hair inside, out of the way. 'We're going to win all our remaining matches and the Belles will drop a few points here and there and then we'll overtake them and *we'll* get automatic promotion.'

There was silence. The other members of our team, Ruby, Alicia, Debs, Jo-Jo and Emily, had come over to see what was going on, and they were looking depressed now, too. Grace is our captain and she's great, but Georgie's often the one yelling at us from her goal. She's usually a fantastic cheerleader for our team.

But today, even Georgie didn't sound quite as confident as usual. I'd heard the hint of nerves in her voice, and I could see from their faces that the others had spotted it too.

'Look, let's not wind ourselves up before the game's even started,' I began as calmly as I could. I wanted to say a lot more, but there wasn't time just then. The ref wanted to start the match.

We all trooped over to our starting-positions, Jasmin still rubbing her tummy. No one would have guessed from the anxious, depressed looks on our faces that *we* were second in the league with a chance of promotion. In complete contrast, the Pickford Panthers were looking relaxed and casual, laughing and chatting – and they were third from the bottom!

I glanced around at the little groups of supporters standing on the touchline. There was Grace's dad, Mr Kennedy, chatting to Lauren's mum, Mrs Bell, who was as glamorous and beautiful as a film star. She had Lauren's funny little dog Chelsea with her, on a lead. Georgie's dad was there too, along with her oldest brother Adey who was an apprentice at our local professional club, Melfield United. They were standing with Jasmin's mum and Jas's brother Dan, and Mr Fleetwood, Hannah's dad. He'd brought Hannah's grandpa with him.

Everyone had someone there to support them except me.

I had this thought before every single game. I knew it couldn't be helped, and so I just had to do what I always did and stop myself from thinking about it. Usually I managed it successfully. But today for some reason I just couldn't stop thinking about Dad. He'd looked so grey and tired today. I felt guilty about leaving him with Milan, even though Mum must be back by now. *How I wished Dad wasn't ill...*

The first blast of the referee's whistle made me jump. The Panthers kicked off, heading in the direction of our goal, and passing the ball between them quite slickly for a team who were at the wrong end of the league. I stayed back a little, covering Georgie, expecting Debs and Jo-Jo to put a stop to the Panthers' advance towards our goal. But they didn't. Debs slid in for a tackle on the Panthers striker and missed, while Jo-Jo gave a loud shriek as she slipped on a muddy knot of grass and almost went flying. The Panthers striker, a red-headed girl called Violet, looked as if she couldn't believe her luck as she was presented with an almost open goal, just me and Georgie standing in her way.

I went in for the tackle and at the same moment Violet tried to hook the ball away from me and get a shot in. My toe just touched the ball as Violet hit it, sending it spinning in the opposite direction. Horrified, I glanced up just in time to see Georgie diving completely the wrong way. It looked like a goal to the Panthers in the first minute!

But somehow Georgie managed to deflect the ball with her knees, even though she was sprawled on the grass. I sighed with relief as the ball bounced across the pitch and out for a Panthers' throw-in.

'God, that was close!' Georgie gasped as one of the Panthers ran to retrieve the ball. 'What a rubbish start...'

Even though we'd managed to stop the Panthers scoring, it didn't seem to help us settle down. Everyone in our team looked nervous and jittery. When we launched our first attack on the Panthers' goal, it all fizzled out when Hannah tried to pass to Grace, who wasn't expecting the ball. She missed it and it sailed straight past her to a Panthers player. Lauren fought to win it back in midfield and then accidentally kicked it wildly out of touch when she tried to set Jasmin up on a run forward. Ruby clashed heads with Jo-Jo when they both jumped for a header, and near the end of the first half, Jasmin didn't get back into position in time after a free kick, leaving a gap in midfield for the Panthers to sweep through and down towards our goal. We were all playing terribly, and there didn't seem to be any way to get back on track. We only had a couple of chances to score, and Grace was so off-form, she missed both of them.

The Stars were so bad, even Mr Fleetwood,

Hannah's dad, couldn't help yelling at us every now and again. He used to be *really* bad, shouting at Hannah during every game, but he'd quietened down a lot since last year. Not today, though – it was all too much for him!

'Come on, the Stars!' Mr Fleetwood kept shouting, 'You can do better than this, girls!'

The first half finished 0-0. *At least we hadn't gone behind*, I thought gloomily as we went to get our bottles of water.

'We were PANTS!' Georgie moaned as we went to get our bottles of water. 'Complete and total pants!'

'It's the curse of the play-offs,' Jasmin sighed, replacing the ribbon in her hair.

'The curse of the play-offs?' I repeated. 'What are you talking about, Jasmin?'

'The team who are second *never* win the play-offs,' Jasmin explained solemnly. 'They always lose. Two years ago the Allington Angels were second. You know Marie-Jayne Cooper, one of their best players? Well, she broke her leg the day before the play-off final, and they lost.'

'How did Marie-Jayne break her leg?' asked Hannah.

'She slipped on a banana skin in the school

playground.' Jasmin looked indignant as Hannah began to giggle. 'It's *true*.'

'Sorry,' Hannah said quickly, twisting the top off her water bottle. 'It just sounded a bit like a comedy sketch!'

'And you know that last year the Belles were second and *they* didn't win the play-offs either.' Georgie chimed in with more doom and gloom. 'Remember? They only had ten players because Sonia Ali got concussion in the first half when she clashed heads with someone else—'

'Tell me about it,' Ruby murmured, rubbing her ear. 'I think Jo-Jo's head must be made of solid wood.'

'Cheeky!' Jo-Jo retorted.

'The Belles lost six nil in the first play-off and they didn't even make it to the final,' Georgie went on. 'Jasmin's right, the play-offs are totally bad news.'

'Didn't something bad happen to the second-placed team *three* years ago?' Grace asked. 'Weren't they in a minibus crash or something on the way to the play-offs?'

Georgie and Jasmin nodded.

'Yep, that's right,' Jasmin agreed. 'It was the Burnlee Bees. No one was hurt, but they postponed the game and then, when they finally played it, the Bees lost.'

I rolled my eyes.

'I wish I'd never asked!' I exclaimed.

'It's so unfair,' Grace sighed. 'We've been second for most of the season, and yet we might not even get promotion.'

'Where's Lauren?' Hannah asked, looking round.

We'd been so busy listening to Tales of the Terrible Play-offs that we hadn't noticed Lauren wasn't with us. She'd gone over to speak to her mum, and now she came running back to us.

'The Belles are winning against the Fairmount Foxes!' Lauren panted, looking totally annoyed. 'It's three nil to the Belles.'

We stared at her in dismay.

'How do *you* know?' Georgie demanded.

'Remember Manda Redmond, the Foxes goalie?' Lauren explained. 'Well, my mum works with hers, so I got Mum to text Mrs Redmond and ask her.'

'So that's that, then.' Jasmin's shoulders drooped. 'The Belles are going to get automatic promotion, and there's *nothing* we can do about it.'

'Of course there is!' Ria came up behind us at that moment. 'I don't want to hear you talking like this, girls. Everything's still up for grabs, and you just need to get your heads sorted, stop all this defeatist talk and get on with it.'

I glanced round at my team-mates. Despite Ria's words, their faces were still gloomy. Suddenly a picture of my dad looking ill and tired popped into my head. He always made me sit down when I got home after a match and tell him all about it, and I was longing to be able to give him the news that we'd been promoted to the top league. He'd be nearly as thrilled as I was! But that wasn't going to happen at the moment, with everyone feeling so down. I knew I had to do something.

'Ria's right,' I said. Everyone turned to look at me, surprised. 'We're second in the league and we're there for a reason – because we've played brilliantly. The Panthers are near the bottom. We're a much better team than they are. Don't forget, we beat them four nil earlier this season.'

'But the Belles are winning, and we're NOT—' Jasmin began.

'We're still only one point behind the Belles,' I broke in. 'One point – that's all. And we've only played one half so far. We haven't lost to the Panthers *yet*.'

Lauren pulled a face at me. 'But we haven't managed to overtake the Belles in the league all season.'

'So?' I shrugged. 'That doesn't mean anything. We've still got a great chance to catch them up, and if we have to take it all the way to the last match of the season, then we will. But I'm *not* giving up now with everything still to play for. My dad isn't very well, and I'd love to cheer him up by telling him that the Stars have got promotion.'

I don't make speeches like that very often. And I *certainly* hadn't meant to say the stuff about my dad, but it had just slipped out. The girls knew my dad was sick, but I'd never told them exactly what was wrong with him. ME was a hard illness to explain, and even some of our Polish friends couldn't get their heads round the fact that Dad was just 'tired all the time', as they put it. So I just avoided telling people about it, even Lauren, Hannah and the others. It was easier that way.

Now I wished I hadn't said anything at all, but I could tell that speaking out like that had actually shaken my team-mates up a little. Probably just *because* it was so unlike me...

'Everything Katy's said is absolutely true.' Ria

smiled at me. 'You're letting the Belles mess with your heads. Forget about them and concentrate on playing your own game. This is a match you should definitely win.'

'Right, then!' Georgie said as the ref indicated the second half was about to begin. 'Let's do it, guys!'

She sounded much more confident this time, and looking around at the others, I could see their faces brighten a little. We all ran back onto the pitch – which was a complete contrast to the way we'd trudged off so gloomily at half-time.

'Is your dad *very* ill, Katy?' Jasmin asked hesitantly.

'He just gets very tired and he can't do much, that's all,' I replied, but I was glad when the ref blew the whistle for the game to restart. My life was too complicated to explain, and like I told you before, I don't want the other girls feeling sorry for me.

The Stars kicked off, and for a few minutes we passed the ball around in midfield, just finding our feet after the break and getting our confidence back. The Panthers had strolled onto the pitch looking like they thought they might get at least a point from this match, but quickly they began to realise that the Stars' mood had changed. I watched from our half as Lauren sent a low cross flying in across the Panthers' penalty area towards Grace. Grace just failed to get to the ball, and it bounced out for a goal kick. A few minutes later, Jasmin scurried down the touchline, shielding the ball from a Panthers defender, and then whipped it inside to Ruby. Ruby took a shot, but it flew over the Panthers' crossbar. We were getting better every minute.

'The Panthers are starting to look worried,' Georgie said to me as we waited for their goalkeeper to take the goal kick. 'Maybe you should push forward a bit more, Katy. Their strikers aren't as quick as you, and you should be OK to get back to defend.'

I nodded. The goalie had belted the ball out into the midfield, and Emily and a Panthers player were fighting over it. The Panthers girl won and tried to pass it to one of her team-mates, but she fluffed it and the ball ended up at Hannah's feet. Hannah pounced on it and immediately ran forward, sliding the ball out to Lauren. The Panthers retreated as Hannah, Lauren, Jasmin, Emily and Ruby charged forward to where Grace was lurking on the edge of the penalty area.

I ran after them. Now Ruby had the ball and she'd taken it wide, a Panthers player shadowing her every move. The penalty area was full of players from both teams watching and waiting to see what Ruby would do next.

I joined them in the box. A couple of the Panthers players looked surprised and a bit flustered to see me there. Ruby spotted me too, and when she got the cross in, she aimed it in my direction. As the ball zoomed towards me, I suddenly realised that I was taller than all the Panthers players, including their goalie. I just had to time my header properly. And I did! I managed to leap up and make contact with the ball, flicking it past the goalie's outstretched hand and into the back of the net.

'GOAL!' I heard Georgie yell from the other end of the pitch.

The other Stars ran over to me, their faces full of relief as the watching crowd applauded.

'Great stuff, Katy.' Grace gave me a hug. 'You should be playing upfront instead of me and Ruby!'

'You've saved the Stars, Katy!' Jasmin announced dramatically, hanging off my arm.

'We're *all* playing better now, that's the secret,' I said with a smile. 'Now can we just finish this game off and get the three points that we *totally* deserve?'

'No problem,' Lauren said, blowing a kiss at me.

And it *wasn't* a problem! From that moment

on, we completely outclassed the Panthers and we quickly took over the whole game. The Panthers just fell apart, and towards the end of the second half Grace managed to grab another goal with a fantastic shot that whizzed between the legs of the Panthers goalie.

'Two nil!' Jasmin crowed happily as we had a massive team hug after the final whistle. 'If it wasn't so muddy, I'd cartwheel around the pitch!'

'It was all down to Katy giving us that kick up the bum at half-time,' Georgie said, slapping me on the back. 'If it wasn't for you, we'd have lost big-time.'

As we walked off the pitch we passed Lauren's mum, who told us that the Belles had beaten the Foxes 3-2. It was a bit depressing, but it was only what we were expecting anyway.

'Three two,' Georgie repeated thoughtfully as we piled into the changing-room. The Stars Under-Elevens team was playing at home today and they'd won too, so it was noisy in there. 'And the Belles were three nil up at half-time. *Very* interesting!'

'Why?' Jasmin asked, yanking open her locker. She gave a scream of surprise as all her stuff toppled over and fell out onto the floor. The rest of us scooted over and helped her collect up everything.

'Because it means the Belles let the Foxes get back into the game.' Georgie picked up Jasmin's black and pink striped socks and tossed them back into the locker. 'The Foxes are bottom of the league, which means that either the Belles are over-confident about grabbing automatic promotion—'

'Or they had an attack of nerves halfway through the game,' Grace added, retrieving Jasmin's denim jacket. 'You're right, Georgie. That *is* interesting.'

'What are we doing tomorrow?' Lauren asked. 'Do you all want to come to mine?'

A blast of Bollywood film music interrupted our conversation. With another shriek of surprise, Jasmin grabbed her denim jacket from Grace and fumbled in the pocket for her shiny purple phone. But when she finally found it and glanced at the display screen, she let out a loud snort of disgust.

'I knew it!' Jasmin announced, pulling a face. 'It's from Sienna. She always texts me when the Belles have won, just to annoy me. Ooh, I can't *stand* that girl!'

Sienna Gerard – now *that* was a strange story. Sienna had started at Jasmin's school last term. She'd made friends with Jasmin and her schoolmates Izzie and May, and she'd even played for the Stars for a short while. But Jasmin had quickly discovered that Sienna just wasn't the nice, friendly girl that she'd seemed – and it hadn't taken the rest of us long to find that out, either. Sienna had got bored with us and had announced just before Christmas that she was moving teams to play for the Belles! She was doing well, too, from what we'd heard, and seemed to be scoring goals for fun.

Jasmin getting that text from Sienna had just reminded me that I probably had a message, too. I opened my locker and found my phone. Yes, I had a voicemail from Mum. And as I listened, I knew straight away that something was wrong.

'Katy, I'm at the local hospital.' Mum was speaking very fast in Polish. 'Your dad is very ill. Can you come here as soon as you get this message?'

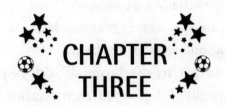

CHAPTER THREE

'Is Tata all right, Mama? What's going on?'

The sign on the wall said not to run down the hospital corridor, but I couldn't help it. I could see my mum sitting in the waiting-room at the end of the corridor, and I dashed towards her as fast as I could. My heart was thundering so hard, I felt sick. I'd never felt so scared in my life. *This was all my fault...*

'It's all right, Katy. He's fine.' Mum grabbed me and gave me a big hug. I almost started crying then, but with relief. 'The doctors are with him at the moment.'

'What happened?' I asked, gulping back my tears as she led me over to a couple of empty chairs. I'd totally lost it when I'd heard Mum's voicemail message. I'd been ready to run out of the changing-room, leaving all my stuff behind, and jump onto the first bus to the hospital.

But the girls hadn't let me.

'What's wrong, Katy?' Hannah had said quickly, after taking one look at my face.

'I have to get to the hospital!' I'd gasped. 'My dad's really ill!' I'd stopped then, staring at them with wide-eyed panic. 'What bus do I get? Does anyone know?'

'Forget the bus.' Grace had taken charge then. 'Get changed, Katy, and me and my dad will give you a lift to the hospital.'

'But—' I began to object automatically, because that's what I always did. What an idiot I am.

'Don't argue, Katy. It's a waste of time.' Georgie began pulling my stuff out of my locker. 'Get changed as fast as you can, you two.'

I'd started pulling off my boots and kit, and Grace did the same. Jasmin and Hannah packed our stuff away in our bags while Lauren and Georgie helped us on with our clothes. In just a few moments

Grace and I were both ready.

'Good luck, Katy!' Jasmin called as Grace and I ran out of the changing-room.

'Hope everything's OK,' Lauren added.

Mr Kennedy had been chatting to Hannah's dad and grandpa when we got outside, but when Grace explained what had happened, he'd packed us into the car immediately and headed for the hospital. I was so nervous, I couldn't say anything except a whispered *Thank you* when we arrived. But Grace had given me a hug before I got out of the car and told me to let them all know how my dad was.

I was lucky to have such great friends.

'So what happened, Mama?' I asked again in a shaky voice. 'This is all my fault. I should never have left Dad on his own.'

'Katy, it's *not* your fault,' Mum replied firmly. 'Dad suddenly had a coughing fit and couldn't breathe. I got home to find Milan trying to make him drink a glass of water, bless him. I ran to the flat downstairs and banged on the door and one of the nurses was there. She rang for an ambulance.' Mum sighed. 'I wish I could speak more English. I could have called for one myself.'

'So Tata's going to be OK?' I asked hopefully.

Mum nodded. 'The doctor told him he has a chest infection and he has to stay in hospital for a few days. But apart from that, he's fine. So don't blame yourself, Katy.' She gave me a hug. 'If anyone's to blame, it's me.'

'Why?' I asked, surprised.

Mum heaved another sigh. I suddenly realised that she was looking very tired and pale herself, and I felt a deep stab of panic. What if Mum got ill, too? How would we cope?

'This is just between you and me for the moment, Katy,' Mum said solemnly. 'I don't want your father to know until he's feeling stronger, OK?'

I nodded, wondering what was coming.

'The cleaning company I work for have just made a lot of staff redundant,' Mum went on. 'So the rest of us are having to do their work, too. That's why I was late home today. And we're not getting any more pay for doing the extra work, either.'

'But that's not fair!' I exclaimed.

'No, and that's not all.' Mum stared wearily at me. 'The managers are saying that the company isn't making enough profit, and we might have to take a pay cut if we want to keep our jobs.'

I felt furiously angry. 'Isn't that against the law?'

Mum shrugged. 'Katy, what can I do?' she said simply. 'If I complain, they'll just sack me too. And I don't know how I'll find another job because my English isn't so great. I'll just have to put up with it.' She slipped her arm around me. 'You're always a big help to me, Katy, but I'll have to rely on you even more from now on. I'm going to be working longer hours, and we might have less money and things will be tough while your dad is so ill. Someone's going to have to look after Milan while I'm working these longer hours and I don't know if your dad will be up to it, even when he comes out of hospital.'

'We'll manage, Mama.' The words were out of my mouth before I even thought about what I was saying. Mum gave me a hug.

'I knew you'd say that, *kochanie*. Now let's go and see your dad.'

As we went down the corridor towards Dad's ward, I couldn't help secretly thinking and worrying about what Mum had said. It sounded like the next few weeks – maybe even months – were going to be difficult.

Already I was always on the run, with one eye on the clock, and now it looked like my life was about to get even more complicated.

'Watch out, Katy. I'm going to eat you! I'm a lion – RAHHHH!'

'Don't eat me, scary lion!' I squealed. Milan roared with laughter and chased me around the living room until we were both dizzy. We were playing zoos. It was Milan's idea, so he got to be all the interesting animals like lions and bears and elephants while I was the boring ones. So far I'd been a rat, a snake and a hippo!

It was Tuesday evening, three days after Dad had gone into hospital. He was still there, but was coming home tomorrow. We couldn't wait to have him back.

The other girls had been *fantastic*. I hadn't been able to make it to Lauren's place on the Sunday, but we'd all been texting each other non-stop and I'd kept them up to date with how Dad was. Then I'd seen Grace, Georgie and Hannah at school on Monday. I'd told them what happened in a bit more detail, but I still couldn't bring myself to tell them *everything*. I didn't say a word about what a rush my whole life was and how my dad was ill *all* the time and couldn't work. Nor did I say anything about Mum's job and the problems she was having and how that was going to affect *me*. I'd already decided that somehow I was going to cope – with school, with football, with helping out at home more and looking after Milan. *Everything*. The Stars had some important matches coming up and I wasn't going to let the girls down, not after all their support. But I'd had to tell them that I wouldn't be at training tonight. Mum would be working, and there was no one to look after Milan except me.

'Right, now I'm going to be a kangaroo,' Milan announced.

'What about me, then?' I asked.

Milan wrinkled his nose. 'You can be...' he thought for a minute. 'A bat!' He burst into giggles as I rolled my eyes melodramatically.

'A *bat*?' I repeated.

'Yes, you can hang upside from the ceiling!' Milan replied with a cheeky grin. 'That's what bats do. Go on, Katy!'

'You little monkey,' I said, smiling at him.

'I'm not a monkey.' Milan was rolling around on the sofa now, almost helpless with laughter. 'I'm a kangaroo!'

'Well, hop over to the front door, then,' I said as

I heard a key in the lock. 'Mama's back from the supermarket.'

Milan leapt up and hopped over to the door. I followed him. I was upset about missing training, although I hadn't said anything to Mum about it. But maybe it was a good thing anyway, I told myself, because I had to get my homework done. I'd started it when I got home, before Mum went out, but I still had loads to do.

'I'm a kangaroo, Mama,' Milan said, bouncing around Mum as she came in with her shopping bags.

'You're the best and most beautiful kangaroo in the whole of Melfield.' Mum dropped her bags and gave Milan a big kiss. I was glad to see she was looking a bit more cheerful, and I guessed she'd spent some time chatting to people at our local supermarket. It stocks the Polish food that we love, like *pierogi, kielbasa* and *ogorki kiszinez,* and also a lot of other stuff from Russia and Eastern Europe. Mum had made friends with some of the other customers who'd come to the UK from Poland, and also from places like Romania, Slovenia and Estonia.

'Everything all right, Katy?' Mum asked as I took the bags from her. 'Are you ready for your training session? You'll be late if you don't leave soon.'

I stared at her in surprise. 'But I didn't think I was going! What about Milan?'

'I met Mrs Zajac at the supermarket, and she offered to babysit tonight.' Mum beamed at me. Mrs Zajac was one of our Polish friends.

'I don't like Mrs Zajac,' Milan said sulkily. 'She smells funny!'

'Oh, dear.' Mum raised her eyebrows at him. 'That's a shame. Because Mrs Zajac bought lots of sweets at the supermarket especially for you.'

'OK, I'll go, then,' Milan said immediately.

Mum bit her lip, trying not to laugh. 'We'll see you later, then, Katy.'

'Thanks, Mama.' I gave her a huge hug and then ran to the bedroom I shared with Milan to pack my kit. My homework books were spread out on my bed, and I pulled a face at them. I'd have to finish the work when I got back from training.

Shouting goodbye to Mum and Milan, I flew happily down the stairs. I *always* felt on top of the world when I had football to look forward to, even if it was just a training session like today. It could cheer me up like nothing else...

As I whizzed outside, I noticed a van parked up

on the kerb, the engine still running. A delivery man was standing at Mrs Jackson's door, waiting for her to open it. I couldn't help staring a bit. The door opened just a crack and I saw Mrs Jackson's hand shoot out and grab the parcel. I don't think she even said thank you. The delivery man looked pretty disgusted, and I could see that he was muttering away to himself as he went back to his van. Forget what I said before about Mrs J not liking us because we were Polish. I don't think she likes *anyone*!

Everything went right for me tonight. The bus was on time and I got my favourite seat at the back and every traffic light was green. I jumped off the bus and hurried through the college to the changing-room. The rest of the Stars team were already there, getting their kit on, and Jasmin, who was pulling down her bright purple tights, was the first to spot me.

'Katy!' Jasmin waddled over to the door with her tights stuck halfway down her legs. I had to laugh as she flung her arms around me. 'I thought you weren't coming.'

'So did I,' I replied. 'But Mum found someone else to mind my little brother.'

'Great stuff,' said Georgie with a huge grin. 'We *need* you, Katy. You're the only reason we got our act together and won on Saturday.'

'Oh, don't be daft,' I said, smiling back at her. 'We were the best team. End of. And no more scary stories about the play-offs, OK?'

'Absolutely,' Grace agreed.

'Actually, that reminds me—' Jasmin began.

With a shriek of protest, Hannah and Lauren both leapt on her and clapped their hands over her mouth. Jasmin fought them off bravely.

'I was *just* going to say that a second-placed team *has* won the play-offs,' Jasmin gasped, still trying to escape from Hannah and Lauren. 'The Emberton Eagles went up to the top league just after I first joined the Stars.'

'So there you are, then.' I began to change into my kit. 'It's been done before – and we can do it again!'

I could *feel* a change in the team as we all ran out of the changing-room. There was a buzz around the training session that wasn't just about us – a couple of the others Stars teams, the Under-Tens and Under-Twelves, were up for promotion in their leagues too, and they already had their heads down and were training hard with their coaches. It was sad that we were coming to the end of another season, I thought with regret, but we still had a chance to make it a really special finish by winning promotion.

Ria started us off with all the usual stuff like slow jogging, high knees, sideways skipping and stretching. Then we did some sprints with and without the ball. We didn't get much chance to chat at first because Ria didn't like us to talk too much while we were warming-up. But later she told us to get into pairs and practise controlling the ball with our first touch. I paired up with Grace while Georgie was next to us with Hannah, and Lauren and Jasmin were on our other side.

'Ria's working us hard tonight,' Lauren commented as Jasmin chipped the ball to her. Jasmin's pass wasn't too accurate and Lauren had to run backwards a little to trap the ball and bring it down.

'Make sure Lauren doesn't have to move to receive the pass, Jasmin,' Ria called. She was down the other end of the pitch with Ruby and Jo-Jo, but she never missed *anything*. 'You should be aiming for the ball to fall right at Lauren's feet.'

'Yes, sir!' Jasmin muttered under her breath, giving Ria a cheeky army salute. Luckily Ria didn't spot *that*.

'So you said your dad's coming home tomorrow, Katy?' Hannah said. I nodded. 'That's fab news.' And she passed the ball to Georgie, who headed it straight back to her.

'Control the ball and keep it in the air at least twice before passing it back, Georgie,' Ria called.

'What does she think I am, a performing seal?' Georgie grumbled.

'Have you got the hump with Ria again, Georgie?' Jasmin asked nosily.

Georgie shrugged. Hannah had passed the ball to her again and she controlled it with her head and flicked it up into the air three times before sending it back.

'I just wish I knew what was going to happen,' Georgie confided in a low voice. 'With Ria and my dad, I mean. Last week I dreamt they got married and I was a bridesmaid – oh my God, it was a *complete* nightmare!'

'Chill, Georgie,' Lauren advised her. 'They've only been going out for a few months, remember.'

'Yeah, well, I wish they'd split up,' Georgie muttered darkly.

'Parents are just *too* much trouble, sometimes,' Lauren sighed, trapping a pass from Jasmin with the outside of her foot. 'My dad's driving me and my mum mad at the moment. He keeps saying we should be saving money because of the credit crunch!'

We all took our eyes off the footballs as they flew through the air and stared at Lauren in disbelief. Meanwhile the balls landed on the grass and rolled *everywhere*.

'Concentrate, girls!' Ria yelled at us.

'But you've got loads of cash, Lauren,' Georgie pointed out as we ran to collect the balls.

Lauren shrugged. 'Dad thinks we should be economising!' she groaned. 'It's doing my head in.'

I smiled a little at the face Lauren was pulling, but secretly I couldn't help thinking that however much the Bells cut down on their spending, they'd *still* be living like celebrities! I imagined inviting Lauren round to our flat, seeing it all clearly inside my head – the battered front door that needed a coat of paint, the shabby carpets on the floor, the small bedroom I shared with Milan... The very idea of the other girls, especially Lauren, finding out that was how I lived made me totally uncomfortable. I was ashamed of myself for feeling this way, but I couldn't help it.

'Well, at least your mum and dad are together, Lauren,' Grace said with a sigh. 'Gemma and I still don't know what's going to happen with our parents.'

'Oh, poor Grace!' Jasmin exclaimed, sending a wild pass towards Lauren that swerved away and almost took Hannah's head off. 'We're all here for you, you know.'

'Thanks, Jas,' Grace said gratefully. 'If I couldn't talk to you guys about it all, I don't know *what* I'd do.'

I was silent as I chipped the ball to Grace. Would it be better if I just came out and told the girls *everything* about my life and why I was the way I was? Why I never had much money to do stuff and why I often had to leave them and shoot off early to go home? They knew bits and pieces about me, like my dad wasn't well and that I had to babysit Milan every so often. But, like I said before, they didn't know what was wrong with my dad or how hard my mum worked and how she didn't speak English, how I had to help out all the time at home and how my life was always rush, rush, rush. And because the girls knew I didn't open up easily, they'd *never* asked why my parents didn't come to watch me play, and why I'd never invited them round to our house. Come to think if it, I don't think they even knew exactly where I lived. The girls always used to offer me lifts home after matches and training sessions, but I almost never accepted, and now they hardly ever asked.

'My parents have got off my case since they accepted that I'm no good at maths and never will be,' Jasmin remarked, collecting the ball from Lauren. 'All I want to do now is overtake the Belles, get automatic promotion and wipe that big fat smug smile off Sienna Gerard's face!'

The rest of us grinned. Jasmin is *so* not a nasty person, but Sienna really did make her life a misery at school and at football towards the end of last term. We were all relieved when Sienna decided to leave the Stars and switch to the Belles.

'Maybe we should introduce Sienna to Olivia, the stepsister from the depths of hell!' Hannah replied. 'They'd probably get on really well – they could swap spells and ride each other's broomsticks!' She sighed. 'It's almost a year since Olivia moved in with us, and we *still* don't like each other that much. Only two years to go before she heads off to uni, though. I can't wait.'

Ria came to check on us just then, so we shut up and concentrated on impressing her with our first-touch skills. All of the girls had problems of various kinds, I thought. It wasn't just me. I felt particularly sorry for Grace – I couldn't *bear* it if my parents split up. But still, that didn't stop me feeling like a bit of an outsider, someone looking at their lives from a million miles away. The girls' parents all had good jobs, they were professional people and they lived in lovely houses. None of them had any money worries. Georgie's, Hannah's, Jasmin's and Grace's families weren't as well-off as the Bells, but they were like millionaires compared to us! My life just felt so different from theirs.

Training finished and we went off to get changed. I was just pulling my jacket on when my phone rang. Remembering what had happened after the match on Saturday, I grabbed it immediately. The display screen said *Mum*, and that made my heart pound with fear.

'Hello, Mama?' I said fearfully. 'What's happening? Is Dad OK?'

'Oh, don't worry, *kochanie*, it's not that.' I was so relieved, my knees went underneath me and I had to sit down on the bench. I saw the other girls glance at each other, concerned. 'It's just—' Mum lowered her voice. 'Maya, the girl I work with tonight, has gone home sick. She asked me not to tell the managers because she's worried they might sack her, so I offered to do all the work myself. But I'm really behind with everything. I'm going to be *hours*.'

I made an instant decision. 'I'll come and give you a hand.'

'Would you, Katy?' Mum brightened up immediately. 'Thank you. It'll be much quicker with two. I've called Mrs Zajac and she doesn't mind keeping Milan till we get home.'

'OK, I'll be there in about twenty-five minutes.'

I rang off and shoved my phone in my pocket. I was very aware that the others were trying to pretend they hadn't been listening, but they were obviously wondering what was going on.

'Is everything OK, Katy?' Hannah asked.

I nodded.

'Would you like a lift somewhere?' Jasmin offered. 'My mum won't mind.'

'No, thanks,' I said quickly. 'It's fine. See you.'

I hurried out and ran for the bus. I knew the girls would probably be discussing me and my strange behaviour now, but I didn't care. It was better than having to explain a whole lot of stuff I didn't want to talk about. And if I'd accepted a lift from Jasmin and her mum, I'd have had to tell them where I was going and why.

The office block where my mum worked on Tuesday nights was huge with what looked like hundreds of windows. I'd been there once before so I knew the way. Mum was standing around in the enormous reception lobby when I arrived, waiting to let me in.

'Thanks for coming, Katy,' she said gratefully, handing me a blue overall. 'I've done all my own work. Now we just have to do Maya's.'

We got down to it straight away, emptying waste bins, wiping desks and computers, clearing up the kitchen area and vacuuming the carpets. Luckily we didn't have to clean the *whole* building, just the offices on the third and fourth floors. But the rooms were so big, there was a lot of running around to do. My legs were already aching a bit from training, but by the time we'd finished all the cleaning, I was ready to *drop*.

Mum and I got the bus home and then went to collect Milan. He'd fallen asleep on Mrs Zajac's sofa, and so he was really cranky when we had to wake him up. I helped Mum get him to the flat and into our bedroom. But my heart sank when I saw my homework stuff still laid out on my bed. Quickly I gathered it up in my arms while Mum tried to settle Milan down. I had an English essay to finish, several pages of maths to do and some reading for my history lesson tomorrow. Yawning, I went out into the living room and sat down on the sofa. It was going to be a long night...

'Katy, we really *should* go to bed,' Mum said just over an hour later. 'Have you got much left to do?'

'No, I've just finished,' I said, quickly, closing my maths book. It wasn't true. I'd finished the English essay and I'd already decided to do the history reading on the bus to school tomorrow. But I hadn't even started the maths. I didn't want Mum to feel guilty though. I said goodnight and slipped quietly into the bedroom. Milan was peacefully asleep, looking adorable.

I waited until I'd heard Mum get into bed and switch out the light. Then I put my torch on and opened my maths book. Hopefully the sums wouldn't take me too long, I thought as I reached for my calculator. If I was lucky, I might get finished soon after midnight...

It was 12.30 am by the time I finally switched off my torch and closed my eyes. I was *exhausted*. But

I wasn't going to give up on everything before I'd even started. It was up to me to juggle school and football and home, and make sure that I did the best I could. Mum and Dad and Milan were relying on me.

But I already knew that if it came down to it, I'd have to choose supporting my family over everything else. And that included football.

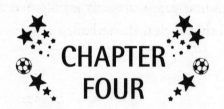

CHAPTER FOUR

'You're going to training tonight, aren't you, Katy?' Dad asked me. He was lying on the sofa with Milan, watching a cartoon.

Surprised, I glanced up at him. Dad had come home from the hospital yesterday afternoon, and we'd had a little party in our flat with some of our Polish friends. Dad looked a lot better now that his chest infection was clearing up, but he was still a bit weak.

'No, of course I'm not going,' I replied. I'd already warned the girls that I wouldn't be there tonight. 'I'm staying here with you and Milan while Mum goes to work.'

After I'd stayed awake till all hours on Tuesday night doing homework, Wednesday had been another manic day. We'd all slept in, even Milan, who usually woke me up at 6.00 am every morning by jumping on my bed! It had been a rush to get to school, although I *had* managed to read my history textbook on the bus. I'd had to run like the wind not to be late, though.

On Wednesday night I looked after Milan while Mum went to work. I was hoping to get my homework done, but it was impossible because Milan kept interrupting me. Mum was late back again because she had so much extra work to do, and although I'd managed to start my homework after putting Milan to bed, I hadn't finished it. I'd had to go through the whole torch routine again, and this time I was up until just after one in the morning. I was feeling a bit tired, I had to admit, however hard I tried to hide it.

'Tata and I have talked about this, Katy.' Mum popped her head out of the kitchen. 'We think you should go. Tata is feeling so much better—'

'And we don't want you to have to give up everything you enjoy,' Dad broke in. 'It's not fair.

We know how important the Stars are to you.'

I hesitated. 'But what if – something happens?'

'I'll call you straight away,' Dad promised. 'I've even taught Milan how to use my phone so he can call you or your mother. Here, Milan.' He took the phone off the coffee table. 'Show Katy what you've learnt.'

Grinning widely, Milan took the phone and pressed a few buttons. The next moment I heard my phone ringing in my pocket.

'Brilliant!' I exclaimed. 'You're such a clever boy.'

'I know,' Milan said casually, and we all laughed.

'So you see, Milan can call if we need you,' Dad said. 'But everything will be fine. You go and enjoy yourself, Katy.'

'Thanks, Tata.' I gave him a hug and scooted off to grab my kit.

'Just make sure you keep your phone with you, Katy,' Mum called after me. 'Don't leave it in your locker.'

'OK,' I called back. I didn't tell her that Ria had a strict rule – NO phones allowed on the pitch at any time, whether it was a match or a training session. But I'd get around that somehow. I already had an idea...

*

'Katy, you've done it again!' Jasmin exclaimed as I hurried into the changing-room half an hour later. 'First you say you're not coming, and then you turn up. What's going on?'

'Well, if you're going to be like *that*, I'll go home again,' I said, straight-faced.

Jasmin gave a squeal of protest, and Grace and Georgie each grabbed one of my arms and hustled me over to the lockers.

'Katy's just playing hard to get!' Georgie said, slapping me on the back. 'She knows how much we miss her when she's not here.'

'Is everything OK, Katy?' Lauren asked, peering at me. 'You look a bit tired.'

'Yep, I noticed you yawning all through art class at school this afternoon,' Georgie added.

'I'm fine,' I said breezily. Of course I was tired, but I'd kept going somehow. I'd helped Mum with the housework when I got home from school, and I'd also cooked dinner while Mum gave Milan a bath. But I'd actually managed to get most of my homework done tonight before I came to training. I could easily finish the rest when I got home without staying up too late. I was looking forward to an early night for a change!

Just before we all left the changing-room, I put my pink hoodie back on over my kit. The hoodie had deep pockets and when no one was looking, I slipped my phone inside one of them. Then I followed the others outside. If Ria heard my phone ringing, I'd simply say I'd forgotten it was in my pocket. Maybe it would just be easier if I explained the whole situation to Ria and the girls, I thought, feeling a bit uneasy. But there was *so* much I'd have to explain, I couldn't face it. And to be honest, I was secretly a bit worried that Ria might think I couldn't cope with all the stress at home. What if she dropped me from the team? I frowned. Or was I just using that as an excuse because I didn't want anyone else to know what my life outside the Stars was really like? I groaned under my breath. All this wondering and thinking about things was driving me crazy.

As Ria got us all warming up, I took my hoodie off and laid it on a nearby bench. I didn't dare keep it on in case my phone fell out of the pocket while I was warming up. I was going to try to make sure that I stayed as close to the bench as possible so I could hear the phone if it rang. But that was a bit difficult at first because Ria wanted us to jog right around the pitch!

'I met Kirsty MacAllister when Gemma and I went into town after school yesterday,' Grace remarked as she ran alongside me.

'The Melfield United player?' Georgie gave a snort of disgust. We were playing Melfield Under-Thirteens this coming Saturday, our last match before the big show-down with the Belles.

'That's her.' Grace turned her head to grin at Georgie. 'She reckons Melfield are going to thrash our backsides on Saturday.'

'She's got a nerve!' Georgie fumed. 'Well, Melfield have got *no* chance of promotion, anyway.'

We were coming around the corner of the pitch, near the bench where my hoodie was lying. I swerved over to the right, as close to the bench as I dared, listening hard, trying to find out if my phone was ringing or not.

'Katy, what are you doing?' Hannah grumbled. 'You just trod on the back of my heels!'

'Sorry,' I mumbled. My phone *wasn't* ringing. I swerved left again to join the others, and Lauren raised her eyebrows at me.

'Have you got ants in your pants or what?' she asked. 'You're dodging around all over the place, Katy.'

'Come on, no slacking, girls!' Ria called from behind us.

'I think Kirsty was deliberately trying to wind me up,' Grace went on. 'She was saying all sorts of stuff about how the Belles are *definitely* going to win automatic promotion.'

'Kirsty's big mates with Lucy Grimshaw, isn't she?' Jasmin asked. Lucy Grimshaw was the Belles' scary striker. She was almost as tall as Peter Crouch!

Grace nodded. 'Kirsty said that Lucy and the other Belles are dead confident about beating us the week after next, too. Apparently Sienna Gerard said she's going to score a hat-trick against us.'

'Oh!' Jasmin gasped, outraged. 'That is just *so* typical of Sienna!'

'I know we haven't got an easy game this week against Melfield,' Lauren remarked. 'But neither have the Belles. They're playing the Angels, and they're a *really* good team.' The Allington Angels were third in our league and seven points behind us.

'The Angels might nick something from the Belles,' Georgie said thoughtfully. 'Let's hope they can get a point, at least. And if we can beat Melfield, then we'll go ahead of the Belles. Result!'

'I'd *lurve* to see Sienna's face if that happened!' Jasmin said wickedly.

We ran on in silence for few a moments, and then we were coming around the corner of the pitch towards the bench again. I tried to slide over towards it so that I could listen out for my phone. But I didn't realise Georgie was so close behind, and she bumped right into the back of me.

'What are you doing, Katy?' she complained, poking my shoulder. 'You're supposed to be going forward, not sideways.'

'You keep staring at the bench over there,' said Hannah curiously. 'What's the matter?'

'Nothing!' I spluttered, swerving to avoid Jasmin, who'd suddenly stopped dead.

'Sorry,' Jasmin apologised, 'My lace has come undone.' And she hobbled over to the bench. I watched in alarm as she prepared to plonk herself down dangerously close to my hoodie – and my PHONE!

'Don't sit on my hoodie!' I yelled. A vision of Jasmin's backside crushing my phone to bits and Dad being ill and Milan not being able to call me ran through my head in about two seconds flat.

Jasmin had just been about to sit down, but now she leapt up again as if she'd been scalded.

'Oh! What did I do?' she gasped.

'Um – nothing,' I said quickly, feeling like a total *idiot*. 'It's OK.'

Looking a bit wary, Jasmin sat down on the other end of the bench as far away from my hoodie as she could get, and began to re-tie her lace.

'Katy, you're acting really crazy tonight,' Georgie said as we ran on. 'What's going on?'

'Nothing!' I snapped. I was more angry with myself than with the girls, really. *Why* hadn't I just told them in confidence that I'd had to bring my phone with me? Why did I always have to keep everything secret, just because I didn't want them to know all about my real life?

After warming up, Ria got us working in a big circle, practising passing to each other, so I was able to make sure I stood quite close to the bench. Then Ria took Georgie and the goalies from the other teams down to the other end of the pitch to do some goalkeeping drills while Danny MacDonald, the Under-Twelves coach, kept an eye on us. That was great for me because Mac was watching his own team *and* us, so he was too busy to notice that I kept wandering casually over to the bench to check if my phone was ringing or not.

Towards the end of the training session, Georgie and Ria came back, and we finished off with a six-a-side game – me, Grace, Jo-Jo, Alicia, Georgie and Lauren against Jasmin, Debs, Emily, Alicia, Hannah and our occasional sub, Hattie Richards. I got so into the game, I kind of forgot about my phone. But just after Grace hit the ball into the net past Hannah, who was goalie for the other side, I heard a familiar noise…

MY PHONE WAS RINGING!

I almost jumped out of my skin. Nervously I whipped round to glance at Ria, who was watching us play. Ria wasn't standing near the bench, but my phone sounded deafening! Had she heard it? I didn't think so, but Lauren, who was near me, was looking worried.

'Go and get that, Katy, before Ria hears it!' Lauren whispered. 'I'll distract her!'

As I backed away towards the bench, Lauren charged across the field after the ball. Then she gave a yelp of pain and fell dramatically onto the grass.

'Lauren, what's wrong?' Ria called, running over to her. So did the others.

'I have CRAMP!' Lauren shrieked at the top of her voice, easily drowning out the sound of my phone. 'Ooh, it's so PAINFUL!'

I grabbed my hoodie, hoping Ria didn't spot me as I pulled my phone out of the pocket. I saw Grace looking at me, though. She saw the phone in my hand and moved quickly to stand behind Ria, shielding me from Ria's gaze.

It was Mum calling.

'Katy, sorry to disturb you,' Mum said. She sounded stressed. 'Have you finished training?'

'Almost,' I replied. 'Where are you?'

'I'm still at work.' Mum sighed deeply. 'It's going to be another late one, Katy, because I've been given extra stuff to do.'

'I'll get changed and be right there,' I broke in. 'Don't worry, Mama. I'll help you get it all finished.'

Mum tried to object, but I told her I was coming anyway. I said goodbye and rang off, just as Lauren climbed to her feet. My phone was back in my pocket before Ria even turned around.

'Great session, girls,' Ria said. 'I know you're going to do well against Melfield United this Saturday. Now off you go and relax until then.' Ria's sharp dark eyes were suddenly fixed on me. 'Especially you, Katy. You're looking a bit washed-out.'

'I'm OK,' I said quickly, hurrying off the pitch.

I had to get changed as fast as I could, and then go into town to the offices to help my mum with the cleaning. Then we had to get home and I'd have to finish my school work, even if I only managed to do the stuff that was due in tomorrow. My face fell at the thought of yet another late night.

'What was all that about, Katy?' Georgie asked bluntly as we went into the changing-room. 'Lauren said your phone was ringing inside your hoodie.'

'So *that's* why you yelled at me when I went to sit down!' Jasmin exclaimed, her eyes wide. 'Why did you have your phone with you?'

'Oh, it's not important,' I muttered. 'Thanks for covering for me, Lauren.'

'No probs,' Lauren replied. 'But you could have warned us. We only want to help, Katy.'

'Yes, we don't want you to get in trouble with Ria,' Hannah added.

'And Ria's right, Katy.' Grace was staring closely at me. 'You *are* looking tired.'

I felt dead embarrassed. And *stupid*, because I hadn't told them.

'Look, there's nothing wrong,' I said impatiently. God, I know when I'm in this mood that the more people want to help, the more I want to stand on my own two feet. I'm pricklier than a hedgehog sometimes, and I'm *so* not proud of it. But it's just the way I am. 'Everything's fine. *I'm* fine. Now can we just leave it and get changed, please?'

None of the girls said anything else, not even Georgie. Hannah changed the subject and began to talk about the match against Melfield on Saturday, and the others joined in. I kept my head down, worrying about how I was going to get through the next couple of weeks until the end of the season. Once we'd played our last match – and hopefully got promotion – I'd have loads more free time. All I had to do was hold things together until then.

It couldn't be that difficult. Could it?

I sat at the living-room window, looking anxiously outside. It was Saturday morning, the day of the Melfield United game. Dad had had a bad night, and was now asleep on the sofa. Mum didn't want to leave Milan with him while I went to the match, so before she went to work, she'd arranged for her best friend Magdalina to look after Milan. But Magdalina was late, and I couldn't leave until she arrived.

Yawning, I glanced at the clock. I still had time to

make it to the game – *if* Magdalina arrived in the next five minutes. It was an away game so I had to get into town to the Melfield United training ground where the match would be played. It was a slightly longer journey for me than if we were playing at home, so I was already wearing my kit under my coat to save time when I got there.

'When's Magdalina coming?' Milan asked. He was being quiet – for once! – looking at some dinosaur picture books we'd borrowed from the library.

'Ssh, don't wake Tata,' I warned him. 'Magdalina will be here any minute now.'

I hoped.

On Thursday after training I'd gone to help my mum finish her cleaning job again, and then it was back to the flat to carry on with homework by torchlight. I'd had real problems with a French comprehension exercise, and hadn't got to sleep until after 2 am. So on Friday morning I was almost asleep on my feet. I had a strong cup of coffee at breakfast which perked me up a bit – like most Polish people, I love strong coffee! So I was feeling a bit brighter by the time I got to school. I was OK all morning. Georgie, Grace and Hannah *did* say that I looked a bit tired, but I laughed it off. The trouble was I had a big lunch – fish and chips, my favourite! – and it was a sunny afternoon for March and the classrooms were lovely and warm, and I was sitting next to a hot radiator during our history lesson, which was all about the industrial revolution, and REALLY boring. So was it any surprise that my eyes started to close?

I don't think I could have been asleep for longer than a few minutes. Then I felt someone poking my arm.

'Katy!' It was Georgie, who was sitting next to me. 'Wake up!'

I didn't want to wake up at all, but I knew I had to. I forced my eyelids open to find Mrs Stewart still droning on about factories and machinery and everyone taking notes except me. Georgie and Grace, who sat the other side of her, were staring at me, wide-eyed.

'I didn't even notice you were asleep, Katy,' Grace whispered. 'Georgie heard you snoring!'

I blushed with embarrassment. 'Thanks for waking me, guys.'

'Here, copy my notes.' Grace passed her book over to me. 'My writing's easier to read than Georgie's scribbles!'

'True,' Georgie agreed. 'So what's happening, Katy? How come you're so tired?'

'It's nothing.' I shrugged Georgie's questions off with a smile. 'I'm just not sleeping that well at the moment.'

'No talking, please,' Mrs Stewart said sternly, so we had to shut up then. Which had been a relief for me, at least...

Another three minutes had gone by, and I was still staring out of the window and there was *still* no sign of Magdalina. Maybe she wasn't coming, I fretted. I'd have to ring Ria very soon to see if she could get Hattie Richards to take my place.

Still, at least I'd got most of my weekend homework out of the way already, I thought with a sigh of relief. I'd had to miss seeing the girls last night, though, to get it done. We always met up on Friday evenings the night before a game, but getting my homework out of the way had been more important this time. Now I was free to help Mum with the shopping, cleaning and cooking all weekend because she was exhausted too, with all the extra hours she was working. I guessed that Grace and Georgie had told Hannah, Lauren and Jasmin all about how I'd fallen asleep in the lesson, though, because I got a whole heap of texts asking me if I was OK. I made a joke of it, as usual, sending them a smiley face to pretend that I was all right. But I did feel tired out, and I wasn't doing a very good job of hiding it either.

Suddenly I jumped to my feet with a sigh of relief. Magdalina was hurrying up the road with her three young children, two of them in a double buggy and her daughter Ania, who was the same age as Milan, walking beside her. I waved at Magdalina and she waved back.

'Magdalina's here, Milan,' I said, grabbing his jacket. 'Come on.'

'Sssh! Don't wake Tata!' Milan scolded me.

I rolled my eyes, which made him giggle, and helped him on with his jacket, gloves and hat. Quickly I checked that Dad's phone was on the coffee table next to him, as well as a fresh glass of water. Then Milan and I tiptoed out.

'Sorry I'm a bit late, Katy,' Magdalina said as we joined them outside. 'It was a nightmare getting this little lot ready! We're going to the park, Milan, so you hold Ania's hand and look after her, OK?'

'OK,' Milan said proudly.

'Thanks, Magdalina,' I said. 'See you later.'

As I rushed off down the road, I glanced at my watch. I wasn't sure if I'd make it to the bus stop in time. I could catch the next bus, but then I might not get there for the start of the game.

When I arrived at the stop, though, there was a crowd of people waiting. It was obvious from their annoyed faces that the bus was late. Ten minutes later, it still hadn't arrived.

'I bet it's been cancelled,' one woman grumbled to her friend.

I bit my lip. This was all I needed! I made a quick decision and dashed off down the road again. I could get a different bus into town from a stop about ten minutes' walk away – or five minutes if I ran all the way. This bus wouldn't drop me so close to the Melfield training ground, though, and I'd have a ten-minute walk at the other end, too. But maybe one of my team-mates might spot me on the way and offer me a lift, I thought hopefully. For once I did think of texting Grace or Hannah or one of the others and asking them to pick me up. But I'd left it too late now. Silly me...

I made it to the stop in record time, but although there was a queue, there was no sign of the bus. I wondered if it was stuck somewhere because the traffic heading into town was *really* bad. Time was ticking away, I thought anxiously, staring at my watch again.

'Katy!'

A familiar voice shouting my name made me jump. I glanced up and saw Ria in her black sports car, crawling along in the slow traffic. She'd wound down one of her electric windows and was beckoning to me.

'Jump in!' she called.

Thankfully I left the bus queue and did as she said, settling myself down in the cream leather passenger seat.

'You're as late as I am, Katy,' Ria remarked, tapping her fingers impatiently on the steering-wheel. 'The traffic's hellish. I think there's some sort of protest march going on in the town centre today, and the police have closed off some of the roads.' She shot me a sideways glance. 'How are you? You've been looking tired at training recently.'

'Fine,' I said, hoping that Ria wasn't about to start grilling me about what was going on at home. 'I'm OK, *honestly*.'

'Glad to hear it,' Ria replied, her eyes on the road. 'I know being a defender isn't one of the glamour jobs, Katy, but you're very good at it. The whole team is really built on you at the back and Grace up front. You only joined last year, didn't you? So you should be very proud of yourself.'

I turned pink. I was embarrassed but pleased. Ria didn't say things like that very often, and I knew she meant it. I *had* to make sure I didn't let her or the other girls down.

When we arrived at the training ground, though, everything was in a right mess. Lisa King, the Melfield Under-Thirteens manager, was waiting for Ria as we drew into the car park. She looked stressed and worried.

'A couple of my girls haven't made it yet, and three or four of yours aren't here either,' Lisa told Ria as we got out of the car. 'I think they must be held up in traffic.'

'Well, maybe we can start the game a little later,' Ria suggested. 'We'd better clear it with the ref.'

Lisa pulled a face. 'The ref's late because of the traffic, too!' she explained. 'I just got a text from her.'

Leaving Ria and Lisa to sort things out, I hurried across the car park to the away changing-room. Debs, Jo-Jo, Emily, Alicia and Ruby were all there and so was Lauren.

'Oh, Katy, you made it!' Lauren exclaimed with relief. 'Jasmin's here, too—'

'Hi, Katy!' Jasmin called from the toilets.

'But I just got a text from Georgie, and she and her dad are stuck in the traffic,' Lauren went on, 'I don't know *where* Hannah and Grace are.'

Right on cue, Hannah dashed through the door, her long stripy scarf flying out behind her. At the same moment Jasmin bounced out of the toilets and they crashed right into each other.

'Oh!' Hannah gasped as Jasmin gave a squeal.

'Take it easy,' Lauren said anxiously. 'We can't afford any injuries – we're already one player down until Georgie gets here.'

'We won't be starting on time anyway,' I said as Grace came running in. 'The ref's not here yet either!'

Everyone was *so* depressed as the kick-off time came and went without Georgie *or* the ref turning up. Jasmin couldn't sit still and kept pacing up and down the changing-room in a panic, which didn't help. The longer we sat there, the more tired I began to feel. I couldn't remember a time when I'd been this exhausted before. I was secretly worried it might affect my game.

Finally Georgie arrived, red in the face with

frustration and moaning about the traffic jam. She was followed a few minutes later by the ref. As we all lined up at the changing-room doors, ready to file out onto the pitch, I was alarmed to find that my legs felt so heavy, I could hardly pick them up. To be honest, all I wanted to do at the moment was go home and *sleep*. Maybe I'd be OK once I got out into the fresh air.

The ref was keen to start the game quickly and was urging us to get into position straight away. As I walked down the pitch with Georgie, I spotted Kirsty MacAllister, the Melfield player Grace had mentioned meeting in town last week.

'We're going to mash you into little bits today, Jasmin,' Kirsty was saying gleefully as Georgie and I passed by. 'And the Belles are sure to beat the Allington Angels, so then you'll have *no* chance of catching them up, and they'll get automatic promotion.'

Jasmin pulled a face at her. Georgie stopped dead, glaring at Kirsty, and I stopped, too.

'Look, we *know* you're big mates with Lucy Grimshaw and some of the other Belles,' Jasmin said with a sniff. 'But you don't have to be *quite* so childish, Kirsty.'

'Yeah, if you love the Belles so much, why don't you go and play for them?' Georgie asked. 'Oops, I forgot – you're just not good enough, are you?'

Kirsty stopped smiling then and stalked off across the pitch.

'She tried out for the Belles a few years ago, but they turned her down,' Georgie told me.

'I bet Sienna Gerard scores a hat-trick for the Belles against the Angels today,' Kirsty called back over her shoulder. 'Sienna's *such* a great player. If she'd stayed with your team, maybe you'd be top of the league instead of second!'

Jasmin scowled at her.

'Don't let her wind you up, Jasmin,' I said. 'She's doing it on purpose.'

'I know,' Jasmin replied, hopping impatiently from one foot to the other. 'God, I just feel so *bleurgh*! Everything's gone wrong this morning, hasn't it?'

I knew what Jasmin meant. This was such an important game and because the day had got off to a bad start, everyone was nervous and wound up and on edge, even Melfield, who had nothing to play for except three points.

The ref was looking flustered, too. She blew the

84

whistle for the Stars to kick-off the game, and we lost the ball immediately in mid-field before we'd even got anywhere. Emily went in to try to win it back, and she hassled the Melfield player so much she fumbled her pass and accidentally sent the ball spinning over to Grace. Grace turned to make a run forward. But then a Melfield defender I hadn't seen before went charging in and sent Grace flying.

'Oh!' Grace gasped out in pain as she hit the ground. To be honest, the Melfield girl looked just as shocked by her clumsy tackle as Grace and the rest of us were.

'I'm *so* sorry!' the Melfield defender said over and over again. She was almost close to tears as the ref, who was obviously in a bad mood herself, spoke a bit sharply to her.

Luckily Grace was all right, just a little shaken up. But that incident in the first few minutes made everything *worse*. Lily Adams, the girl who'd chopped Grace down, was quite an awkward and clumsy defender who couldn't tackle to save her life. None of us Stars wanted to go anywhere near her. Lauren was floored a few times, too, and I could see her getting *really* stressed about it. I hoped desperately that Lauren wouldn't lose her temper, because when she gets going, she's even worse than Georgie!

I could see too that Kirsty MacAllister was taking every opportunity to wind Jasmin up whenever she got near her. I couldn't hear what Kirsty was saying, but from the look on Jasmin's face, it wasn't very nice.

Towards the end of the first half, Melfield got a corner. Hannah, Jasmin and Emily came into the box to help defend, while Lauren stayed back with Grace.

'Concentrate!' Georgie urged us as Rhiannon Marsh, one of the Melfield midfielders, took the corner.

The ball swung in, swerving a little in the breeze, and headed straight for Jasmin. Looking flustered, she tried to bring it down neatly, but she made a mess of it and knocked it straight into the path of the Melfield striker, Verity Blaine. It was a simple tap-in for Verity, and she rolled the ball over the line before Georgie could do anything about it.

1-0 to Melfield.

The Melfield girls celebrated like *they* were the ones in with a chance of promotion. Meanwhile, Jasmin was nearly in tears.

'Sorry!' she gasped. 'That was all my fault.'

'You shouldn't have let Kirsty wind you up, Jas,' Georgie muttered, collecting the ball from her net and booting it savagely downfield.

Half-time couldn't come quickly enough for me. My legs were aching and I felt so tired, I could hardly move. Ria came over to tell us that the Belles and the Angels were 0-0 at half-time, so that gave us a bit of a lift. But as we walked back onto the pitch for the second half, I was wondering again how I was going to cope.

'You'd better stay back, Katy,' Georgie said as she took up her position in goal. 'Don't go running forward too much.'

I stared at her in surprise. 'Why not?'

'Because you're dead on your feet!' Georgie retorted with a frown. 'You can hardly keep your eyes open.'

'That's not true,' I snapped.

Georgie shrugged. 'Whatever,' she said, rolling her eyes.

Embarrassed and upset, I hurried into position for the kick-off. *Everyone was irritable and out of sorts today*, I thought glumly. And I shouldn't have snapped at Georgie like that, because I knew she was right. I *would* stay back, like she'd suggested.

The second half was just as bad-tempered and hard-fought as the first. But somehow the Stars managed to up their game just a little, thanks to Grace, who tried her hardest to make the most of every single scoring chance she got (which wasn't many). Melfield began to crack up and break down a little as the Stars increased the pressure. And *finally*, Grace managed to score after a great pass from Ruby sent her free and on-side, with only the goalie to beat.

One all, with around five minutes to go.

The Stars didn't even have time to celebrate Grace's equaliser properly. We knew we *had* to get a winner to keep up with the Belles. So for the last five minutes we all dashed forward, even me with my aching legs. We bombarded Melfield's goal with shots of all kinds, trying to get that vital goal. Lauren went close with a free kick, and Ruby almost headed one in, but it flew past the post.

It was still 1-1 when the whistle blew.

'Oh, well, we did our best,' Hannah said, trying to put a brave face on it as we shook hands with the Melfield team.

'Sorry for being cranky earlier,' I said to Georgie.

'Me, too.' Georgie threw her arm around my shoulders. 'It was that kind of game, wasn't it?'

'Bet the Belles have beaten the Angels,' I heard Kirsty MacAllister whisper teasingly to Jasmin. 'That means they'll be three points ahead of you now.'

'Oh, go and jump off a cliff somewhere!' Jasmin retorted, walking away from her.

Suddenly Ria came racing across the pitch towards us, phone in hand. She looked incredibly excited.

'Girls, the Belles lost!' she exclaimed.

'What?' Georgie shrieked. 'Say that again, Ria?'

'The Belles lost to the Angels,' Ria repeated. 'One nil! You know what this means, girls?'

'Ooh, quick, somebody do the maths and tell me!' Jasmin squealed. 'My mind's gone blank!'

'It means we're level on points with just our match against the Belles to go,' Grace gasped, her eyes shining. I sighed with relief. I'd been *so* worried because I knew my poor performance today hadn't helped the team at all – and now here we were being handed another chance for automatic promotion, despite our awful performance. It was unbelievable!

'WHOO-HOO!' Jasmin yelled, leaping onto Grace and hugging her to bits. All the other Stars, including me, surrounded them and joined in until we were just one huge, whooping, cheering mass of girls, jumping up and down like crazy!

'Just remember that the Belles have a better goal difference than us,' Ria said with a smile. 'That means we *have* to beat them next week.'

'We're going to mash them into little bits!' Jasmin declared, shooting a triumphant glance at Kirsty MacAllister. She was hurrying off the pitch looking extremely embarrassed.

'Course we will,' Georgie said. 'Won't we, guys?'

Everyone agreed loudly with more whoops. I joined in, but secretly I was wondering what kind of state I was going to be in by next Saturday. I was tired out already, and I had another hard week ahead of me.

I would have to be at my very best against the Belles. And at the moment, I had to admit that wasn't looking at all likely.

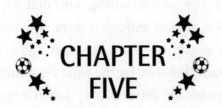

CHAPTER FIVE

I could hardly wait to get home after the game and tell my mum and dad everything that had happened. I got changed in double-quick time and dashed off, even though the other girls were still celebrating.

'Hang on a sec, Katy,' Hannah called after me as I went over to the changing-room door. 'We haven't decided what we're doing tomorrow yet. Are we all meeting up as usual?'

'Hope so,' Lauren said in a muffled voice as she pulled her Stars shirt over her head.

'Just text me,' I said, giving them all a goodbye wave.

'Yeah, but will you come?' Georgie said, kicking off her boots. 'You've been totally difficult to get hold of recently, Katy.'

'I'll do my best,' I promised. 'I've got stuff going on at home. Text me, OK?'

And I hurried off. I was really looking forward to telling my parents everything, and that had given me a real boost, even though I was still tired. I even managed to run for the bus when I saw it coming! Mum would be home by the time I got there, and the four of us would have a cosy lunch together – we always had home-made soup and rye bread on Saturdays – and I would tell them all about the game.

But as I reached our front gate, I stopped dead. I stared at the house next door, Mrs Jackson's house. The front door was ajar...

I frowned. That seemed *really* odd to me. Mrs Jackson didn't even go out that much, so why was the door open? Wondering what was going on, I hung around there at the gate for a few minutes in case Mrs Jackson came and closed it. But she didn't.

Oh, God, I didn't know *what* to do. I mean, why should I bother about Mrs Jackson? She'd only ever been grumpy and off-hand with me, hardly even saying hello to me when I spoke to her. And I was *dying* to run upstairs and tell my family all about the game.

But somehow I just couldn't. Not until I found out if Mrs Jackson was OK.

I opened Mrs Jackson's gate and went up the front path. Then I hovered a bit nervously around the open front door for a few minutes, listening hard, but I couldn't hear any noise inside.

What if Mrs Jackson had gone out, and there was a burglar in there?

Taking my phone out of my pocket, I clutched it firmly so that I could ring for help if I had to.

'Mrs Jackson?' I called.

No answer.

I pushed the door open a little wider. 'Mrs Jackson?'

Still no answer. So I stepped through the door and into the hall, my heart thumping away like crazy.

Suddenly a door further down the hall swung open.

'Aaargh!' I screamed loudly, taken totally by surprise.

Mrs Jackson let out a shrill shriek, too. We'd nearly frightened each other to death!

'What are you doing in my house?' Mrs Jackson demanded, quite rudely, I thought, since I'd been prepared to save her from burglars! 'How did you get in?'

'Your door was open,' I explained, 'I was worried about you.'

'I'm fine,' Mrs Jackson replied abruptly. 'I probably didn't close the door properly and it just popped open. It's done that before.'

We stared at each other for a moment.

'Well, I'd better be off,' I said at last. 'Sorry I scared you.'

'It's all right,' Mrs Jackson muttered, looking a little ashamed of herself, would you believe. 'Well, thank you for checking.' Which was better than nothing, I suppose, and more than I was expecting. Feeling a bit awkward, I hurried outside again.

I let myself in at our front door and ran upstairs. My mum was cooking vegetable soup for lunch, and the flat felt warm and homely. Milan and Dad were sitting on the sofa, reading the dinosaur books together.

'How did the match go, Katy?' Dad asked eagerly.

'We won and the Belles lost!' I declared dramatically, flinging my bag onto the floor. 'We're level on points with only our game against the Belles to go.'

Dad's tired face lit up. 'I knew you could do it!'

'Yippee!' Milan yelled. He jumped off the sofa and insisted on presenting me with his old teddy bear as a reward.

'But not to keep,' he added anxiously, 'Only to *borrow*.'

Mum came out of the kitchen, wanting to know what was going on, so then I had to tell them everything about the game. They were all so interested and excited, that I forgot what had happened with Mrs Jackson. It was only when we were sitting at the table with steaming bowls of vegetable soup and plates of buttered rye bread in front of us that I remembered.

'Mrs Jackson seems rather an unhappy person,' Dad remarked after I'd told them what happened. 'I feel a little sorry for her.' That's typical of Dad. He always tries to think the best of people.

'Yes, but I was only trying to help,' I said. 'She could have been a bit nicer.'

'She *did* say thank you,' Dad reminded me.

'I was at the supermarket today, and I was chatting to some of the other customers in the coffee bar there.' Mum frowned at Milan, who was carefully collecting every piece of carrot from his bowl of soup and placing it on his side plate. 'One

95

of them, Elizabeta, knows Mrs Jackson a little because they go to the same doctor, and she told me that Mrs Jackson lost her husband quite recently.'

'Oh.' Now I felt *bad*. 'So she's all on her own?'

'No, she has a grown-up son, but he lives on the other side of town,' Mum explained.

'Perhaps Mrs Jackson is lonely without her husband,' suggested Dad. 'That could be why she's a little grouchy.'

'Well, if she was a bit friendlier to everyone, maybe she *wouldn't* be so lonely!' I pointed out, slurping down another spoonful of soup.

Mum tipped some of the carrots back into Milan's bowl. 'Just eat a few of them, sweetie.' Then she glanced at me again. 'I was thinking about baking murzynek tomorrow. I could make two, and you could take one over to Mrs Jackson, Katy. Just to be good neighbours.'

'OK,' I muttered reluctantly. Murzynek is a traditional Polish cake with a rich chocolate glaze, and it's totally yum – far too good for Mrs Jackson!

Still, Mrs Jackson wasn't my problem, was she? I was having a fab-u-lous weekend so far! I'd made it to the match, thanks to Magdalina, we were level on points with the Belles and we had the BIG game against them next week to decide who was going to get automatic promotion. AND I'd nearly finished all my weekend homework. Yay for me!

By Sunday morning, though, I'd started to come back to earth a bit. For once, Milan didn't wake me up early by dive-bombing me, but I woke up at 5 am and couldn't get back to sleep, even though I was tired out. How stupid am I? I just couldn't stop my brain whizzing round, thinking about school and the girls and the Belles match next Saturday and wondering how Dad was going to be feeling today. And the more I tried to tell myself to go to sleep, the more wide awake I felt. Crazy!

Then, later that morning, I got a text from Lauren that upset me a little.

Hi K, meeting @ leisure centre @ 2pm for swim, can u come??? L x

Well, the short answer to that was – no, I couldn't. The leisure centre, which is on the other side of town, is fantastic and it's *so* much nicer than the local council-run pool. But it costs a lot to get in, and I can't afford it every time the other girls want to go because I have to get two buses as well. At the moment, with my mum worried about losing her job, I just *couldn't* ask her for any money.

As I messaged Lauren back to say that I wouldn't be going, I felt very sad, as well as a little jealous. I *hated* feeling that way, but I couldn't help it. I often felt like an outsider because the other girls had so much more than I did. Bigger houses, holidays, more clothes, shoes, make-up and everything else.

Don't think that those things are more important to me than my dad, mum and Milan because they're *not*. But it would be so satisfying, just once or twice, to be able to do all the things the others did without counting every penny. And best of all, I'd love to be able to treat the girls to something – even if it was just ice-creams all round – to thank them for being such cool friends. But most of the time I could barely afford even to buy an ice-cream for *myself*.

'Are you meeting up with the others this afternoon, Katy?' asked Mum, whisking the eggs into the cake mixture. We were together in the kitchen and I was helping her make the murzynek, one for us and one for Granny Grumps (Mrs Jackson!). Dad and Milan were in the living room playing a game of Snakes and Ladders that Mum had bought cheap in a charity shop.

I shook my head. 'Not today,' I said casually.

I was standing at the oven with my back to her, stirring milk, sugar, cocoa powder and oil on the hob. 'I've got some homework to finish.'

Mum lowered her voice. 'I haven't said anything to your dad yet about all the problems at work,' she murmured. 'I've just told him I'm covering extra hours for people who are off sick. I don't want him to worry. But I'm quite excited, Katy, because I might have the chance of another job!'

'Really?' I stopped stirring and turned to glance at her. 'That's fantastic news, Mum! Where?'

'At the Polish supermarket.' Mum smiled at me, and I could see she was thrilled. 'The owners, Mr and Mrs Kowalski, don't have a vacancy at the moment, but they've asked me if I can start by covering for staff who are ill or on holiday. The trouble is, I'll have to carry on with my old job for the moment and try to fit in the supermarket wherever I can. It might be at very short notice, too.' Mum stared anxiously at me. 'Do you think we can cope with everything between the two of us, Katy?'

'Of course we can, Mama!' I said confidently. My heart was sinking right down to my shoes, but I didn't allow my doubts to show in my face. If Mum was taking on shifts at the supermarket alongside her cleaning jobs, then that meant more work for me, too, and I was already stretched to the limit... But I *couldn't* let my family down.

'Do you think so?' Mum didn't look that convinced despite my brave tone. 'I've noticed you're already looking tired—'

'I'm fine,' I broke in. 'The football season finishes in the next week or two, and then it's the Easter holidays. I'll have a good rest, then.'

Mum nodded, seeming satisfied. But inside I was already panicking. I *had* to be at my best for the game against the Belles next week, but at the moment I could hardly keep my eyes open and my legs felt *so* heavy. Even taking the murzynek over to Granny Grump's house was an effort – although that could have been because I expected her to bite my head off when I offered her the cake!

It wasn't *quite* that bad in the end, but it wasn't that great, either. Holding the plastic container with the cake inside, I rang Mrs Jackson's doorbell. A moment later I saw the net curtains at the living-room windows twitch, and I knew Mrs Jackson was peering out at me. Would she open the door or not? She did – but only about ten centimetres wide!

'Yes?' Mrs Jackson asked abruptly.

'My mum and I have been baking murzynek,' I explained. I took the lid off the container and showed her. 'It's Polish chocolate cake. We thought you might like to try it.'

Mrs Jackson stared suspiciously at the cake like she thought it might be full of poison or something!

'Well, I *am* quite capable of making my own cakes,' she muttered a little ungraciously. 'I'm not a charity case, you know.'

God, I felt like chucking the murzynek at her, to be honest with you!

'We just thought you might like to try it.' I held the plastic box out to her and to my surprise, she took it. ''Bye for now.'

As I hurried back down the path, I *think* I heard Mrs Jackson say *thank you*, but I might have been imagining it!

Honestly, what's wrong with her? I thought, rolling my eyes. *Can't she tell the difference between people being kind to her and being treated like a charity case?*

My phone buzzed then and when I read the text from Lauren, I forgot all about Mrs Jackson. The girls had decided not to go to the leisure centre and they were meeting up at Lauren's place instead. That meant I could go along, too. Result!

Imagine the most beautiful, airy, spacious house you can think of, filled with expensive furniture and pictures, with a huge conservatory of tropical plants looking out over an enormous, landscaped garden with a hot tub in one corner. Well, that's what Lauren's house is like. Whenever I went there, I *knew* I could never, ever invite the girls round to our tiny, shabby little flat. The Bells weren't snobby, but they had this gorgeous house and two posh cars and they even had a housekeeper, a lovely Slovakian lady called Tanya. Honestly, I felt like a humble peasant whenever I visited Princess Lauren's palace!

It was Tanya who opened the door to me when I arrived.

'Hi, Katy,' she said in Slovakian. Tanya and I sometimes speak Slovakian and Polish to each other, because the two languages are very similar and so we can understand what the other person's saying. Isn't that cool? 'The girls are in Lauren's room. They're expecting you, so go straight up.'

'Thanks,' I replied in Polish, 'see you later.'

I went up the sweeping mahogany staircase that was like something out of a Hollywood film set and along a wide corridor lined with plush cream-coloured carpet. As I got closer to Lauren's bedroom, I could hear shrieks of laughter and little woofs from Lauren's dog, Chelsea. What *were* they all up to?

I opened it and went into Lauren's gorgeous, stylish cream and purple bedroom. I swear that the whole of our flat would fit into her room, it was so big! Lauren has everything that anyone could ever want in a bedroom – her own flat-screen TV, a DVD player, a laptop, a phone and a huge bed piled with silk and satin cushions. Is it really horrible of me to admit that, even though I love Lauren to bits, I'm just a *teeny* bit jealous of her?

Grace, Jasmin, Hannah, Georgie and Lauren were all crouched on the floor around Chelsea and seemed to be trying to persuade her to stand up on her hind legs.

'Hello, you guys,' I said, 'what's going on?'

'Oh, hi, Katy.' Lauren grinned at me as Chelsea waddled over to say hello. She rolled over and I tickled her fat little tummy. 'We're just trying to train Chelsea to do some cheerleading for the Belles match next Saturday. She *is* our official mascot, after all.'

'It's my birthday next week, and I can't even *think* about it until the Belles game is over,' Hannah groaned.

Jasmin was staring at me a bit intensely, I thought.

'So how're you, Katy?' she asked.

'Fine,' I replied, feeling rather surprised. And of course, right at that minute, I *would* feel a great big yawn coming on! I just about managed to stop it by clamping my lips together. I definitely didn't want the others to realise how tired I was feeling.

'That's *great*,' Jasmin said enthusiastically. 'We're *really* pleased to hear it!'

'Why?' I knew I sounded a bit defensive and prickly, and I could see that Hannah and Grace were now shooting warning looks at Jasmin. Maybe the others had guessed I wasn't one hundred per cent at the moment, I thought guiltily. But I did *not* want to talk about it right now.

'Hey, watch this, Katy,' Georgie added quickly, obviously determined to change the subject. 'Who's the best team, Chelsea?' she asked, holding out a doggy treat. 'Is it the Springhill Stars?'

Chelsea growled menacingly, and all the girls collapsed into fits of laughter except for Georgie.

'No, Chelsea, you're supposed to bark for the

Stars and growl at the Belles!' Georgie complained, whipping the treat out of reach as Chelsea lunged for it. 'Not the other way round!'

Chelsea looked puzzled.

'She needs a lot more practice,' Grace remarked.

'What do you think of the Belles, Chelsea?' Jasmin asked.

Chelsea barked happily and Georgie groaned, turning to Lauren.

'I thought you said this dog was mega-intelligent?' Georgie grumbled. Then, while she wasn't looking, Chelsea leaned forward and snatched the treat from Georgie's hand with her teeth. We all fell about, laughing hysterically as Chelsea crunched the treat at lightning speed and swallowed it down. The shocked look on Georgie's face was *so* funny!

'Told you Chelsea was intelligent!' Lauren spluttered. She could hardly get the words out, she was giggling so much.

'Maybe we could dress Chelsea up in a Stars kit,' Hannah suggested. 'I know she always has a purple ribbon tied to her collar for matches, but if we could get a mini Stars shirt for her, how cool would *that* be?'

'Very cool,' said Grace. 'I've got some old Stars shirts at home from when I was younger. Maybe we could cut one down to make it fit Chelsea.'

'Won't Chelsea mind?' I asked.

'No way,' Lauren said, 'She's already got a princess outfit and a ballet tutu and a pink romper suit and she *totally* loves wearing them, don't you, Chelsea? She's a diva at heart!'

'Just like her owner,' Georgie snapped back, quick as a flash. Lauren's response was to grab a heart-shaped purple cushion off her bed and whack Georgie around the head with it. Instantly we all piled in and got stuck into a cushion fight!

Even while I was battering Jasmin with a big cream cushion and she was begging for mercy, I was thinking how much I *love* the girls. The fact that I hadn't told them all about my home life was nothing to do with them and the kind of friends they were. It was all about *me*, and my daft pride. Jasmin, Hannah, Lauren, Grace and Georgie were almost as important to me as my family were, and I really didn't want to let any of them down.

But I had a sick, nervous feeling in the pit of my stomach as I thought about the week ahead. It would be exhausting and difficult getting through my homework and helping my mum and looking after Milan. And then, at the very end of the week, there was the *massive* game against the Belles.

Would I be able to cope?

Or would it all be too much?

I could only wait and see.

CHAPTER SIX

Tuesday night training two days later, and I could hardly keep my eyes open. Not good.

Ria had got half of the team to stand in a big circle and had given them a ball each. The rest of us, including me, were inside the circle, where we had to run around as fast as we could, collecting passes from the girls on the outside and returning them accurately. Most of my energy – the bit I had left, anyway – was taken up with trying to stop myself yawning. I'd already mis-hit several of the return passes, and now, as Hannah slid the ball towards me from the outer circle, I sliced wildly at it. The ball flew high up into the air and then dropped down like a stone, right towards Georgie's head. But Georgie was so intent on pass and return, she didn't even notice.

'Look out!' Jasmin shrieked, pulling Georgie aside in the nick of time. The ball sailed past Georgie's ear and hit the grass. Georgie nearly jumped right out of her shorts!

'Where did *that* come from?' she demanded.

'Sorry, Georgie, that was my fault,' I muttered, feeling like a right idiot.

'Concentrate, girls!' Ria called. But I *couldn't*. My head ached and my brain felt like it was stuffed with cotton wool, and my legs and feet didn't seem to be working properly. It was hard just to put one foot in front of the other, never mind make an accurate pass! I sucked my cheeks in as another jaw-breaking yawn threatened to overwhelm me.

Earlier this evening I'd dashed home from school to cook dinner and babysit Milan because my mum had been offered her first shift at the supermarket. Then I'd dropped Milan at Mrs Zajac's because Dad was having one of his bad days and couldn't look after him. After that I'd raced for the bus – and missed it, getting to training late and already tired out. I knew that Mum would be late for her cleaning job, too, because of doing the shift at the supermarket, so I was planning to go and help her at the offices after training finished. Oh, and did I mention that I still had some homework to do after we'd picked up Milan from Mrs Zajac and got home? I'd managed to get my maths done on the bus home from school, but it was going to be another night of me and my torch under the duvet...

'I had a terrible dream last night,' Jasmin confided in us as we went to get changed after training finished. 'I dreamt the Belles beat us ten nil, and Sienna scored all ten goals.'

'Nightmare!' Lauren groaned.

'Exactly!' Jasmin agreed. 'I couldn't get back to sleep for *ages*.'

I tensed up because I was expecting someone – Georgie, maybe, because she was never shy about holding back! – to comment on how tired *I* was looking. But no one did.

'I was awake for ages, too,' Grace sighed. 'Mum and Dad had an argument last night when Dad dropped me and Gemma off after school. I think the chances of them ever getting back together are as small as me winning *The X Factor*. Meaning, less than zero.'

'I'm so sorry, Grace.' I linked arms with her and gave her a comforting squeeze. A huge yawn took me by surprise then, and I couldn't help letting it out, almost cracking my jaw in the process! To my surprise, though, none of the girls made any kind of comment about it – which I thought was a bit strange, considering we'd just been discussing not sleeping very well. I was relieved, though.

After training, it was more rush, rush, rush. First, to the offices to help Mum finish off the cleaning, then home to pick up Milan. Quick bath and bed, and then English, science and geography under the duvet by torchlight. My grades at school hadn't started to suffer yet, thank goodness, but I knew it was only a matter of time before they did. All I had to do was get through the next week or so until the football season finished, I kept telling myself, and then I'd have loads more time. So it was even more important to me that we beat the Belles and clinched automatic promotion this weekend. Otherwise we'd go into the play-offs and that meant two extra matches right at the end of the season. I could hardly get out of bed in the mornings these days as it was – two more matches would just about finish me off!

Somehow I struggled through Wednesday at school, and then I got the bus straight to the offices to help Mum with the cleaning. She met me in the lobby as usual to let me into the building, but I was surprised to see she had Milan with her.

'Mrs Zajac's ill and Magdalina's gone back to Poland to see her parents,' Mum explained. 'Your dad's asleep, so I had to bring Milan here.'

'I'm bored!' Milan grumbled loudly.

'Come on.' I took his hand. 'I'll find you something to do while Mama and I get on with the cleaning.'

I sat Milan down at one of the desks on a swivel chair, so turning around and around amused him for about a quarter of an hour. Then I found him some paper and pens and left him drawing pictures of dinosaurs. But when I went back to check on him a few minutes later, I found him munching an apple!

'Where did you get that apple from?' I asked.

'I found it on the desk,' Milan replied, taking another huge bite.

'Milan's nicked someone's apple!' I groaned to Mum, trying not to laugh.

Mum looked worried. 'I hope they don't complain to my bosses tomorrow,' she muttered.

'Oh, nobody would complain about losing an apple!' I said quickly, wishing Mum didn't look so anxious whenever she mentioned the company she works for. I was *so* hoping that Mr and Mrs Kowalski would offer her a full-time job at the supermarket, and then she could leave.

When we got home, there was a shock waiting for us. As I followed Mum and Milan through our gate, Mrs Jackson's door opened and she popped out, looking a little embarrassed. She had a blue cake tin in her hands.

'Thank you for the chocolate cake, these are for you,' Mrs Jackson said in one huge breath. Then she thrust the cake tin awkwardly at me.

'Er – thank you,' I said, feeling a bit uncomfortable.

'What is it?' Milan jumped excitedly around me. 'Open it, Katy, open it!'

I flipped the top off the tin, and inside was a pile of crumbly, golden, home-made cookies.

'Yummy scrummy!' Milan exclaimed, his eyes wide. 'Mama, can I have one, please?'

Mum nodded. She gave Milan a cookie and then nudged me.

'Ask Mrs Jackson to come up to our flat for a cup of tea,' she said in Polish.

'*What?* You've got to be joking!' I replied, also in Polish, which was lucky, because Mrs Jackson couldn't understand what we were talking about. But I think she might have guessed from the horrified look on my face!

'Just ask her, Katy,' Mum said sternly.

'Um – my mum wants to know if you'd like to come and have a cup of tea with us,' I mumbled.

'Oh, no, there's no need for that—' Mrs Jackson began.

'Please come,' Milan said earnestly, smiling widely at her and showing off his cute dimples. 'Please, please, please, please, please.'

Not many people can resist Milan when he's in that mood! I actually saw Mrs Jackson's face soften as she stared down at him.

'Well, all right,' she agreed. 'But I can't stay long.'

Great! I thought. But of course I didn't say that. I didn't need to say anything at all, though, because not only did Milan chat to Mrs Jackson all the way up to our flat, he also insisted on holding her hand! Mrs Jackson didn't seem to mind too much, though.

Dad was awake now, but he still looked tired. He brightened up when Mum explained to him in Polish that our next-door neighbour had come to visit. I felt a bit guilty then for not wanting to invite Mrs Jackson round because I knew Dad got bored being in the flat so much, and he *loved* meeting new people. As I helped Mum make tea and put the cookies and some of our leftover murzynek on plates, I could hear Dad talking to Mrs Jackson. At first her replies were a bit stiff and awkward, but she soon warmed up when Milan kept chattering away to her. He was telling her lots of facts about dinosaurs, and what he didn't know, he made up!

'So your son lives over the other side of town?' Dad was saying to Mrs Jackson as Mum and I brought the tea in. 'What does he do?'

'Adrian's a lawyer,' Mrs Jackson replied with a proper smile. There's a first time for everything, I guess! 'He's married to a very nice girl, Colette, and I have two grandchildren. Edward's six and Stella's about the same age as Milan.'

'Will Stella be my friend?' Milan asked solemnly, putting a small plastic dinosaur toy on Mrs Jackson's knee.

'I'm sure she will, Milan,' she said. I could see

from the look on her face that she was half in love with Milan already!

Dad took a sip of tea. 'Do you see them often?'

Mrs Jackson looked rather uncomfortable. 'Quite often,' she mumbled. 'Actually, after my husband died, they asked me to go and live with them. But I didn't want to be a burden and, besides, I can look after myself. I don't want to be a nuisance. I'm a very independent person, you know.'

I rolled my eyes a little as I made my apologies and slipped away to do my homework, taking some cookies and murzynek to munch on to keep me awake. I couldn't understand why Mrs Jackson was being so silly, especially as her relatives sounded lovely and she didn't seem at all happy on her own! *She was letting her stupid pride get in the way of enjoying her life*, I reflected as I started my geography homework. Ooh, that was a bit deep, wasn't it? But it was true!

Anyway, never mind Mrs Jackson, I had other things to think about. Only three more days to go before the big showdown against the Blackbridge Belles! And now I was going to finish my homework and have an early night, then tomorrow I wouldn't be walking around feeling like I could sleep for a hundred years.

Watch out, Belles.

Here come the Stars!

'GOAL!!!'

There was a roar from the Stars, and from the crowd, as Grace smashed the ball past the Belles' goalie and into the net from outside the box. What a shot!

'Two one to the Stars!' I yelled, pounding over to Georgie. We flung our arms around each other and danced up and down in the Stars' goal. Lauren, Grace and Hannah rushed to join us.

'And there's only two minutes left till the end of the game!' Georgie panted. 'Will somebody *please* tell Jasmin to stop doing her maths homework and get her butt back on the pitch?'

'Sorry,' Jasmin called. She was standing on the touchline, scribbling frantically in a notebook. 'I have to finish these sums. But Chelsea's going to play in my place!'

'Woof!' Chelsea agreed. She bounded onto the pitch wearing a purple ribbon tied to her collar and a tiny, doggy-sized Stars shirt.

OK, so now I *knew* I was dreaming! But I didn't

want to wake up. I was having a fantastic, peaceful sleep, and I wanted it to go on for ever...

'Are you getting off here or what, Miss?'

'Uh, sorry ?' I mumbled, reluctantly beginning to wake up. My eyes were so heavy, I had to force them open. I blinked a few times, not sure where I was, and then it hit me.

It was Thursday. I was on my way to training. I was on the bus. I'd fallen asleep!

I struggled to my feet. The bus driver was leaning out of his cab, staring at me.

'Are you getting off here?' he repeated. 'We're at the bus station. We don't go any further than this.'

'The bus station!' I spluttered, absolutely horrified. I'd gone past the stop for the college, and now I was twenty minutes away! I glanced at my watch. Training had started ten minutes ago.

I groaned, really angry at my own stupidity. I hadn't had the peaceful sleep I was expecting the night before, having finished my homework early. Milan had been sick in the middle of the night – from sneaking too many cookies, probably! – and that had woken me up. Then I'd taken ages to get back to sleep, and this morning Mum had insisted that I didn't go to help her clean tonight after training as she was worried about me looking so tired.

'When's the next bus back to Melfield College?' I asked the driver urgently.

'This one'll be leaving here in about ten minutes, when the relief driver arrives,' he replied.

I couldn't do anything except wait, because it was too far to walk. And just to top things off – you've guessed it – the relief driver was late. I finally got to the college with about fifteen minutes of training left.

I didn't bother to change. Clutching my bag, I dashed through to the football pitches at the back and burst out through the double doors. Ria had got the team playing one of our favourite games where we all lined up on the edge of the box with a ball each, and then, when Ria blew her whistle, we *all* had to score as quickly as possible.

'There's Katy!' Lauren yelled, just as Ria let out a shrill blast on her whistle. All the girls turned to look at the very moment they took their shots, and the balls flew *everywhere*. Only Grace's and Jasmin's ended up in the net, I think! I would have found it really funny if I hadn't been so stressed.

'Sorry, Ria!' I gasped, feeling like a total idiot.

'I—' I stopped myself just in time from saying that I'd fallen asleep. 'Um – I had a problem with the bus.' Well, it wasn't *really* a lie, was it?

'Relax, Katy, it's fine,' Ria said reassuringly. 'We're cooling down now, anyway. Grab a drink of water and have a rest on the bench. You look very hot and tired.'

'We were worried about you, Katy.' Jasmin gave me a quick hug. 'Are you all right?'

I nodded. 'Sorry,' I gulped. 'I let you all down.'

'Don't be daft.' Lauren patted me on the back. 'Even if you score three own goals on Saturday, we'll still love you! Won't we, Georgie?'

'Three own goals? Ooh, I'll have to think about that one!' Georgie said, pulling a face. But then she smiled, and I was relieved. Georgie being so relaxed about things was making the whole situation much easier for me. I couldn't understand it though – she was usually so passionate about everything to do with the Stars.

'Don't stress, Katy,' Grace advised me. 'Missing training once is no big deal.'

The girls were being so kind, I actually felt a teeny bit tearful. Especially when I realised that I didn't have any money left to get home because I'd had to pay for a second bus ticket back to the college. So now I had a forty-five minute walk ahead of me.

'Katy, do you want a lift home?' Hannah asked as I walked off the pitch with them after the session ended. 'You still look a bit stressed.'

I hesitated. It was totally tempting not to have to face that long walk, but I felt embarrassed at the thought of Hannah and her dad, in their big shiny new BMW, pulling up outside our shabby old flat. Suddenly an idea occurred to me.

'OK,' I agreed gratefully. 'Thanks, Hannah.'

I saw the other girls glance at each other in surprise and then quickly try to hide it. We all went to the changing-room and I sat on the bench while I waited for Hannah to get dressed. I was a bit on edge because I sensed that the girls were deliberately *not* asking me why I was so late and why I'd suddenly accepted a lift home after always saying no before.

'Will you be able to come to our usual meet-up in the park tomorrow, Katy?' Lauren wanted to know as Hannah stuffed her kit into her sports bag.

'I'll try,' I promised. 'See you later.'

I was still nervous, wondering if Hannah was going to start asking me awkward questions now that she'd got me on my own. But she didn't. We went out to join Mr Fleetwood, who was waiting in the car park, and on the way we talked mostly about the upcoming match against the Belles and a bit about school. In fact, I was so relaxed, I almost forgot about my secret plan, which was to ask Mr Fleetwood to drop me off about five minutes' walk from our flat.

'Stop!' I yelped anxiously, as I suddenly realised we were getting far too close. 'Here is fine.'

'Is that your place, Katy?' Peering out of the car window, Hannah pointed at a semi-detached house with a garage and a pretty front garden.

I almost laughed. 'No, but it's not far from here,' I mumbled, grabbing the door handle. 'Thanks very much.'

'I can drop you right outside if you give me directions, Katy,' Hannah's dad offered.

But I was already out of the car. 'No, don't worry.' I waved quickly, willing them to leave. ''Bye. See you tomorrow, Hannah.'

I dawdled slowly down the road until I saw the car turn around and disappear. Then I hurried home. Tonight I was *determined* to sleep and sleep and not wake up until the alarm went for school.

How boring am I? But I knew I simply *had* to get my act together for the Belles match on Saturday.

Do you want the good news first, or the bad news? The good news was I slept pretty well on Thursday night and for once, Milan didn't wake me up early. I didn't *quite* bounce out of bed when the alarm went off, but I managed to get myself up and dressed for school without a huge amount of effort.

Now for the bad news: my Friday timetable is *deadly*. I have double maths, double French, ICT, geography and science. It's a killer of a day, and at lunchtime, I remembered with a sinking heart, that I'd been so exhausted I hadn't finished my geography homework the other night and it was due to be handed in that afternoon. I gobbled down my lunch, leaving Hannah, Grace and Georgie in the canteen, deep in discussion about the big match against the Belles, and rushed off to the library. I finished the homework just before the bell for the end of the lunch hour rang, but by then I was tired and yawning and I still had an afternoon of geography and science to get through. Somehow I made it without drifting off to sleep. Don't ask me how!

When I'd said goodbye to the others at the school

gates, Georgie had reminded me about getting together at the park tonight. I didn't think I'd be able to go along, but when I'd got home, Dad had said he was feeling OK, and that he could look after Milan for a little while.

'You'll want to talk about the match tomorrow with your friends,' Dad told me. He looked almost as excited about the game as I was! 'Go and enjoy yourself, Katy.'

I was a bit late getting to the park because I peeled and chopped the veggies for dinner before I left. When I arrived, the girls were gathered on our favourite bench near the football pitches. They looked thrilled to see me, which gave me a warm glow inside. They were *honestly* the best friends I'd ever had.

'Hey, you made it, Katy!' Georgie exclaimed, shifting closer to Jasmin, Lauren and Hannah so that I could squeeze between her and the end of the bench. 'Come and sit down.'

'Georgie, you're squashing me,' Jasmin giggled. There wasn't really room for four people, never mind five, on the seat, and Grace was already perched on the arm of the bench.

'Well, we've never had a problem before,' Georgie

said airily. 'Someone's butt is obviously getting bigger!'

We all grinned.

'I'm deadly nervous about tomorrow,' Lauren remarked, handing round a bag of mini Mars bars. 'I won't sleep a wink tonight.'

'Everyone's got to be *totally* up for it.' Georgie eyeballed Lauren sternly. 'And that means getting a good night's sleep and having a proper breakfast.'

'Yes, Mum,' Lauren said, pulling a face at her.

I nodded, agreeing with everything Georgie had said. I would have to bribe Milan not to wake me up early in the morning, I thought. He knew all about how important the match was, so hopefully he'd take some notice!

'Katy, would you like a lift to the game tomorrow?' Grace asked. 'Just in case you have a problem with the buses again.'

'Thanks, but I'll be fine,' I answered quickly. 'I'll leave a bit earlier.' Mum knew how important the game was, so I was confident she wouldn't be late home from work. I appreciated Grace asking me, but it was out of the Kennedys' way, and, besides, I didn't want to be a nuisance...

I smothered another yawn then, turning my head a little so that the others didn't notice. Suddenly,

125

though, Georgie gave a loud yell right next to my ear, and *that* woke me up, I can tell you!

'Look over there!' Georgie exclaimed. 'It's Jacintha, Lucy and Sienna!'

The Belles captain, Jacintha Edwards, their tank-like striker Lucy Grimshaw and Jasmin's ex-friend Sienna Gerard, who now played for the Belles, were heading across the grass towards us.

'What the hell are *they* doing here?' Georgie ranted. 'They *know* we meet in the park on Fridays. I bet they've just come to wind us up about tomorrow!'

'Keep calm, Georgie,' Grace murmured.

'Well, well, well, what have we here?' Jacintha said loudly as they approached our bench.

'I *think* they call themselves a football team,' replied Sienna in that lazy, slightly American drawl of hers. She was stunningly beautiful with her long, ultra-shiny blonde hair and amazingly blue eyes, but Sienna wasn't at all the kind of person I'd want for a friend. She'd made poor Jasmin's life a misery until Jasmin had finally found the courage to stand up to her a few months ago.

'Oh, really?' Lucy Grimshaw raised her eyebrows. 'They look like a bunch of losers to me!'

'Girls, you'll have to try much harder than *that* to

stress us out,' Georgie retorted.

'Yes, we know exactly why you're here,' Jasmin broke in. 'And it's not going to work.'

'Oh, you think we've come on purpose to wind you up?' Sienna looked highly amused. 'The Belles have been top of the league almost all season, and you've never managed to overtake us, and you think we're worried about tomorrow? Get real, Jasmin.'

'Of course you're worried,' Grace replied. 'You must be – you lost your last game!'

Sienna glared at her.

'Oh, by the way, Grace,' Jacintha said casually, 'I thought you might like to know that my brother Nat has got a new girlfriend.'

Grace didn't react at all, but it was totally mean of Jacintha to mention it. We all knew that Grace had had a bit of a thing for Nat Edwards, but that he'd messed her around by chatting up both Grace and her twin sister Gemma at the same time.

'Whoever she is, she's welcome to him,' Grace said coolly, staring steadily at Jacintha. 'Nat wasn't very nice to me, or to Gemma.'

'Must run in the family,' Georgie broke in, glancing frostily at Jacintha. I hadn't said anything because every time I opened my mouth, I felt a yawn coming.

My head was feeling a bit heavy again, and it was an effort to keep my eyes open, so I propped myself up on the arm of the bench, resting my cheek on my hand.

'Well, we mustn't keep you,' Hannah said. 'Goodbye.'

'Oh, I think the Stars are trying to get rid of us,' Lucy remarked. Her voice seemed to be coming from a long way away now, as I felt my eyes close… 'I think we're getting to them, you know, girls. Tomorrow's going to be easy-peasy!'

'Six nil to the Belles!' Sienna added smugly.

'Look, we're all up for this game tomorrow,' Jasmin insisted confidently, 'And nothing you say is going to put us off.'

'Oh, really?' Jacintha remarked, 'Do you think you'll be able to stay awake that long?'

Although I was dozing off by now, I heard the sound of laughter, and then Georgie shook my arm.

'Katy!' she whispered, 'Wake up!'

'Er – wh-what?' I gasped, sitting bolt upright. Sienna, Jacintha and Lucy were absolutely killing themselves laughing! I was mortified.

'Yes, we can see you're *totally* up for it,' Sienna declared, hardly able to get the words out through her giggles.

'Would you like us to ring you all tomorrow morning, just to make sure you get up in time?' Jacintha enquired.

'We are *so* going to win this game,' Lucy said gleefully. 'Automatic promotion is ours, girls!'

And they strolled off again, arm in arm, still laughing.

'Sorry, guys,' I muttered, feeling like a real prize prune. 'I don't know what came over me.'

'Don't worry about it, Katy,' Lauren said quickly. 'If the Belles think we're a pushover, more fools them.'

'Yes, if they're over-confident, that's loads better for *us*,' added Hannah.

'I'm ordering you to have an early night tonight, Miss Novak!' Georgie said teasingly. I was secretly very relieved. Georgie was usually stressed to the max when we had these big games coming up, but she was really chilled about it all at the moment, and that meant I wasn't feeling under as much pressure as I might have been.

The Belles' sarcastic comments had really fired me up though. That night I went to bed when Milan did – at 8.30 pm! I'd already warned Milan not to wake me up early, and he'd promised solemnly that he wouldn't. But about six o'clock next morning, I surfaced to hear him muttering away to his teddy bear.

'We have to be quiet because we mustn't wake Katy up,' Milan was saying in a loud whisper. 'I'll read a story to you.' I heard a thud as he reached for the picture book on his bedside table and dropped it. 'Oops!'

I sighed.

Then the door opened and Mum came in. She was already dressed because she left for work soon after six.

'You go back to sleep, Katy,' she said, tucking the duvet around me. 'I'll take Milan to the offices with me so you can get some peace and quiet. Then you can leave before I get back, too.'

'Thanks, Mama,' I murmured as she whisked Milan out of bed and got him dressed. I don't even remember them leaving the room because I was already fast asleep again.

I woke up feeling better than I had all week. I was actually looking forward to the game. I washed and dressed and had a quick breakfast with Dad, who presented me with a good-luck card Milan had made. It had a picture of a dinosaur in a Stars shirt on the front!

'We'll be thinking about you, Katy,' Dad said when I gave him a goodbye hug. 'I wish I could be there to cheer you on...'

'I'll tell you all about it when I get home,' I promised. Then I grabbed my bag and flew down the stairs and out of the front door. It's amazing what a difference a good night's sleep can make! I was early, too, which meant that if there were any problems with the buses, I'd have time to find a different route, or maybe, if it was an emergency, ask one of the other girls to come and pick me up. But that was a last resort.

Humming to myself, I bounced along the street towards the bus stop. When my phone rang, I didn't think anything of it. I just guessed it was one of the girls calling.

But it wasn't.

'Katy, it's Mama.' The frantic tone of my mum's voice filled me with dread. 'I've lost Milan. He's gone missing!'

CHAPTER SEVEN

I jumped off the bus and ran down the street towards the offices where my mum was waiting for me. The instant I'd got her call, I'd spun round and rushed in the opposite direction without hesitation. I'd had to catch a different bus to get to these particular offices which were right over the other side of town to the college. I'd sat there, almost exploding with impatience as the bus crawled through the Saturday morning shopping traffic. I'd had to take deep breaths to calm myself down because I was in a state of total panic. *Where was Milan?*

'I sat him down at one of the desks, Katy,' Mum had explained, almost in tears, 'and then when I went back to check on him, he'd disappeared. I'm *so* worried he might have got outside somehow and wandered off.'

I tried not to panic. The offices Mum cleaned on Saturday mornings were on the ground floor. So it *was* possible that Milan might have found a way out into the street.

'We'll find him, Mama,' I promised. 'We'll call the police if we have to.'

Mum and I both knew that if her bosses found out, Mum would be sacked because she wasn't supposed to have me or Milan with her when she was working. But that was *nothing* compared to losing Milan... What if we couldn't find him? What if we never saw him again?

I had to focus hard on practical stuff to put those horrifying thoughts out of my head. I'd left the house early, so I might just make it to the game on time if Mum and I found Milan quickly. I pulled out my phone and wrote a text to Ria, telling her I was on my way but that we had a family problem, and I might be a bit late. Could Hattie Richards stand in for me, please, until I got there?

As I sent the text, I silently prayed that Hattie would be available, otherwise I would have abandoned the Stars to face the Belles with just ten players. I felt sick at the thought. Then I sent messages to Lauren, Jasmin, Hannah, Grace and Georgie, telling them the same thing. I got instant replies telling me not to worry, and to call if I needed a lift to the game from *anywhere*. Even if the match had already started, they'd get one of their parents to come and pick me up. God, I could have burst into tears right there on the bus. I couldn't believe how generous they were being to me when I was letting everyone down.

When I reached the offices, Mum was waiting for me. She'd been crying, I could tell, because her eyes were red-rimmed. We fell into each other's arms and hugged.

'Oh, Katy, I'm sorry to call you,' Mum said in a trembling voice, 'I know you were on the way to your football match, but I didn't know what else to do. I'm so afraid Milan might have got out of the building, and then he could be *anywhere*.'

'Let's look around inside first,' I said. 'And if we can't find him, then we'll have to call the police.'

Mum nodded. Together we went back into

the huge, open-plan office and my heart sank as I realised just how many possible hiding-places there were.

'Where was Milan when you last saw him?' I asked.

Mum pointed at one of the desks. 'I left him there.'

I went over to the desk and saw a half-chewed toffee and a picture of two dinosaurs, coloured in with crayons. The crayons were now all over the floor.

'You don't think—' Mum had to swallow before she could get the words out. 'You don't think someone's *taken* him, do you, Katy?'

'Like who?' I replied quickly, secretly dreading that this was exactly what had happened. 'There's no one here today except cleaners. Milan must have wandered off somewhere. I'll help you look for him.'

Mum and I began to search the office, looking under desks and inside cupboards, and calling Milan's name. But he seemed to have vanished into thin air, and there was no sign of him. I tried to keep calm for Mum's sake, but I was becoming more and more worried. And every so often, I couldn't stop myself from glancing at the clock, counting down to the start of the Belles' game. *All the girls would have arrived by now and be getting changed*, I thought as I searched the office kitchen. Fifteen minutes later I checked the time again. Now the match would be starting and everyone would know that I wouldn't be there to play the first half. Would I make it for the second? I had no idea, but it didn't look like it.

I could only hope that Ria had managed to get Hattie Richards to play, but neither she nor the girls had texted me back to say that was the case. I had a horrible feeling that probably Hattie couldn't play for whatever reason, and that the Stars were starting the game with only ten players. *The Belles would absolutely* love *that*, I thought, chewing at my lip as I imagined Sienna Gerard's smug, self-satisfied face. But there was nothing I could do about it. Milan was more important to me than anything, and I'd known all along that if it came down to a choice between football and my family, then I'd *always* choose my family. But I hated letting the girls down.

'That's it, then.' Mum's face was dead white as she joined me at the desk where she'd left Milan. 'Katy, we'll have to call the police.'

With a sigh, I slumped down in the chair where

Milan had been sitting. 'I just don't think Milan would have gone outside,' I said. 'I wonder if he's playing a joke by hiding from us.'

'But he wouldn't hide for *this* long.' Mum looked very distressed. 'He's been gone for nearly an hour, Katy.'

From the chair, I glanced around the room, looking at exactly what Milan would have seen while he was sitting there himself. Suddenly, tucked away in the corner, I spotted a door I hadn't noticed before. It was closed.

'What's in there, Mama?' I asked, pointing at the door.

'Oh, that's the photocopying room,' Mum replied, 'but Milan can't be in *there*. It's kept locked at weekends.'

I jumped up from the chair and went over to the door. I pressed the handle right down, and the door opened. Mum looked startled.

'I didn't even try that,' she confessed, 'I just assumed it was locked, like it always is.'

I pushed the door open a bit wider. 'They must have forgotten to lock it last night.'

'But surely Milan's too small to open that door by himself,' Mum argued, hurrying to join me.

The room wasn't very big, but it had a large photocopier as well as a couple of computers, scanners and printers set up on a desk.

'I don't think Milan's here, Katy—' Mum began. But suddenly I clutched her arm.

'Look, Mama!'

A little blue and white trainer was poking out from behind the photocopier. We rushed over there and peered behind it. There was Milan, wedged into a small space, fast asleep. As we stared down at him, gasping with relief, his long, dark eyelashes fluttered, and he woke up.

'Hello,' Milan said cheerfully. 'I was hiding! You didn't find me for ages, did you?'

'No, we didn't!' Mum replied, hauling him out from behind the photocopier. 'That was very naughty, Milan. We were *so* worried about you.'

Milan's bottom lip began to wobble dangerously. 'I was just playing a joke,' he explained tearfully. 'Then I got tired and went to sleep.'

'How did you open that door?' I wanted to know.

'I stood on my tiptoes!' Milan replied proudly. 'I'm a big boy now.'

'Didn't you hear us calling you?' Mum asked sternly, but she couldn't resist giving him a hug.

138

Neither could I. We were just *so* relieved that he was safe and well.

'No.' Milan shook his head. 'Can I have fish and chips for lunch?'

Mum glanced at me and we had to laugh. Then the clock on the wall caught my eye. The first half was about to start, but I might *just* make it for the second half if I ran for it.

'Good luck, Katy!' Mum shouted after me as I rushed out.

I shot out of the office block like I'd been fired from a cannon. Katy the Human Cannonball, that's me! Then I hurtled towards the bus stop.

'Sorry!' I had to gasp several times as I dodged past people with shopping bags. I was weaving around the passers-by like a skier on a slalom course.

I could see the bus stop ahead of me now. Thank goodness it was a home match for the Stars today, I thought as I waited impatiently for the bus to arrive. If we'd been playing at Blackbridge Community College, it would have taken me an extra ten minutes or so to get there.

I must have glanced at my watch about a hundred times before the bus arrived five minutes later. I jumped on and bagged a seat right by the doors, so that I wouldn't waste any time getting off when we reached the college.

'Come on, come on,' I muttered under my breath as we lumbered along the road, stopping and starting every few minutes because there was so much traffic. I swear, there was almost steam coming out of my ears as we kept pulling in at bus stops to pick up more people. At one stop, *six* people got on the bus, and one of them, a woman, started arguing with the bus driver about the correct fare. I was so stressed out by this time, I almost jumped up and offered to pay her fare myself!

At last, though, we reached the college. I was first off the bus and within about thirty seconds I was racing through the college gates and across the car park. I couldn't decide whether to go and get changed first, but glancing at my watch, I could see that the first half was nearly over so I wouldn't be able to join in anyway. I'd made it for the second half, though, and I was determined to do my *absolute* best.

As I rounded the corner of the college building and headed over to the football pitches, I could hear applause and yells of encouragement from the watching crowds. There were three of the Stars teams playing at home today, but I only had eyes for one game. The Stars Under-Thirteens against the Blackbridge Belles, which was taking place on the pitch furthest away from me.

I ran towards them, trying to pick out the Stars players, although I was still too far away to see very much. Also, there was quite a big crowd watching that game – more people than usual – and I could only catch glimpses of the action between all the people standing around there. I could see Hannah's and Lauren's parents together in one group, with Chelsea on her lead, wearing her mini Stars shirt! And there was Jasmin's mum and her sister Kallie. All three of Georgie's brothers, Jack, Luke and Adey, were standing with Mr Taylor, Georgie's dad, and Mr Kennedy, Grace's father.

As I got closer, though, I could see more of the game through a gap in the crowd. There was Sienna racing down the wing, blonde hair flying, the ball at her feet. She was one of the fastest players I'd ever seen, and there was no one to stop her as she headed straight towards the Stars goal. I could see Georgie moving around, her eyes fixed on Sienna as she tried to narrow the angle for the shot.

Lucy Grimshaw was lurking in the box, towering

over everyone else, although Jo-Jo and Debs were keeping a sharp eye on her. I guessed, though, that Sienna wouldn't pass to Lucy. Sienna was an excellent player, but she was selfish. She wouldn't give the ball away even to her own team-mates, if she thought there was even a slim chance she might score herself.

Sienna cut inside and charged towards the Stars goal, preparing to take a shot. Suddenly I gasped with relief as I saw the tall, lanky, red-headed figure of Hattie Richards, our sub, come up alongside Sienna and hook the ball neatly away with her foot. It rolled out of play for a throw-in to the Belles.

I can't *tell* you how happy I was! Hattie was here and playing for the Stars, so I hadn't let them down as badly as I thought I had. At least they had eleven players. And now I was back, although if Ria felt Hattie should carry on with the game in my place, then of course I wouldn't argue. I'd just stand on the touchline and cheer myself hoarse for the Stars!

I wanted to ask someone what the score was, but I didn't know any of the people in the crowd near me. They must have been the Belles' family and friends, and I was a bit worried that the Belles might be winning, so I didn't want to ask any of *them*!

I did recognise Sienna's mum, Mrs Gerard, looking totally OTT in high heels and a fake fur coat. (At least, I hope it was fake.) But I didn't want to ask *her*, either.

Quickly I glanced around for Ria. She was standing in her usual place near the halfway line, on the same side of the pitch as me. As the Belles set up another determined attack, I hurried towards her.

And that was when my heart just *dropped*...

Lauren was standing next to Ria. She wasn't on the pitch. Why not?

I stopped, frozen to the spot with anxiety, my eyes flicking over the pitch as I counted up the Stars players, one by one. Georgie in goal, Debs, Jo-Jo and Hattie at the back. Emily, Alicia, Hannah and Jasmin, with Grace and Ruby upfront.

The Stars only had ten players on the field.

Now that I looked more closely, I could see that the Stars were in a complete mess. Georgie was gritting her teeth in frustration as Hannah lost the ball in midfield to Sonia Ali, and the Belles surged forward again. Jasmin was looking clumsy and awkward, almost tripping over her own feet as she chased helplessly after Sonia, a sure sign that she was stressed. Even cool, calm Grace looked anxious and restless as she hung around the centre circle. I hadn't seen her even get *near* the ball since I'd arrived. And Ruby, our other striker, was right down the other end of the field, helping to defend.

As a fierce shot from Lucy Grimshaw whistled past Georgie's post, I rushed towards Ria and Lauren.

'Oh, God, I'm *so* sorry I'm late!' I gasped, knowing that this was all my fault. If I hadn't been delayed, Hattie could have taken Lauren's place and we'd still have had eleven players. 'I couldn't help it, honestly, I couldn't. My little brother went missing and we couldn't find him and—'

'Chill out, Katy,' Ria broke in quietly, 'these things happen. At least you're here for the second half, and then we'll be back to eleven players.'

'Are you OK, Lauren?' I asked anxiously.

'I just twisted my ankle slightly a little way into the first half.' Lauren pulled a face. 'It's not too bad, but I can't walk on it very easily at the moment.'

'So the Stars have been playing for almost the whole of the first half with just ten players?' I gasped. So far I'd avoided asking the question because I was dreading what the answer was going to be. But I *had* to know, so I braced myself for bad news. 'What's the score?'

'Three nil to the Belles,' Lauren replied gloomily.

'Three nil!' I repeated, feeling worse than *ever*. I'd been hoping for 1-0. I could have lived with 2-0. But 3-0 just seemed like a huge mountain to climb, especially against a team as good as the Belles. 'This is all my fault—'

'No way!' Lauren exclaimed, slinging her arm around my shoulders. '*You* didn't know I was going to twist my ankle, did you? Like Ria said, stuff happens.'

There was applause from the crowd as the Belles went close again, this time Sonia Ali heading over our crossbar.

'Who scored?' I asked. I had a feeling Sienna would be one of them.

'Lucy got one, and so did Sienna,' Ria replied, her eyes fixed on the action. 'And Debs gave away an own goal. It wasn't her fault, though. There was a real scramble in the penalty area, and she was just unlucky.'

'Georgie's made about five brilliant saves so far,' Lauren added, 'Otherwise the Belles would have a much bigger lead.'

The Stars had the ball in midfield, but they'd lost it again and Sienna was off like an Olympic sprinter towards our goal. I glanced at the ref, *willing* her to blow her whistle and end the half.

A few minutes later, she did. But not before the Belles had got a corner and almost grabbed another goal. It was only a brilliant tackle from Jo-Jo that prevented Lucy Grimshaw from slamming the ball past a helpless Georgie and into our net.

The Belles bounced happily off the field towards their manager, shrieking with laughter and chattering away excitedly. They were so up, it was almost unbearable to watch. Meanwhile, the poor old Stars trudged wearily towards Ria, Lauren and myself, looking fed up, exhausted and totally depressed. I felt terrible. And although I don't cry very often, I could honestly have burst into tears right there and then at the sight of Jasmin's downcast face.

'I'm so, *so* sorry,' I muttered to Grace and Georgie, who reached us first. 'If I could have been here on time, I would. But I just *couldn't*—'

'Forget it, Katy.' Georgie forced a smile as she grabbed a bottle of water. 'You've got to do what you've got to do. No worries.'

'Don't be nice to me, Georgie,' I said shakily. 'It makes me feel worse.'

Grace didn't say anything. She simply gave me

a sympathetic hug, and I could have *howled*.

'You *are* going to play in the second half, aren't you, Katy?' asked Jasmin. Her kit was really muddy, and I guessed she'd tripped and fallen over quite a few times!

'You're joking, right?' I said. I was feeling all fired up now. 'Of course I'm going to play!'

'Don't you think you'd better go and get changed, then?' Hannah said with a smile.

'Oops, yes!' I exclaimed. 'And I'm *really* sorry about getting here so late—'

'Just go!' Lauren interrupted.

I shot off across the pitch, into the college and down the corridor to the changing-room. There wasn't much time before the second half started, and I was determined to be on time for *that*.

Quickly I stripped off and jumped into my kit. Then I went over to the mirror to tie back my hair. I could see I looked paler than usual and I still had dark circles under my eyes, even though I'd had quite a lot of sleep the night before. The last few weeks had left me feeling drained and washed-out and exhausted. But now I had to pull myself together and help the Stars to turn this game around.

Because whatever the other girls said, and despite

how nice they were being to me, I knew that this *was* all my fault.

And now I had to try to put things right.

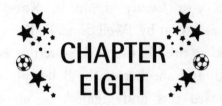

CHAPTER EIGHT

I went back out onto the pitch just as the teams were getting into position for the second half.

'Let's go for it, Katy!' Hannah said urgently to me as I ran past her. 'We're so far behind now, we haven't got anything to lose.'

We gave each other a high five and I hurried on towards our end, where Georgie was already stationed in the goalmouth. On the way I happened to pass Sienna, and I couldn't help staring at her. Honestly, apart from her kit which was hardly muddy at all, you'd never have guessed she'd just played the first half of a football match! Her blonde hair was piled up on top of her head and fixed in place with sparkly pink combs, and she was wearing make-up, too – eyeshadow, mascara, lipstick and blusher. We were supposed to take off all our jewellery before a game, but Sienna was wearing gold hoop earrings and a twisted gold chain.

'Oh, so you *finally* made it, Katy!' Sienna exclaimed as I went by. 'Well done. Did you sleep in? You looked *so* tired in the park yesterday evening!'

Sonia Ali and another of the Belles players, Alex Lowrie, heard this and giggled. I longed to say something cutting in reply, but I bit my tongue. I knew that was *exactly* how Sienna got to people, and I wasn't going to let her put me off.

The ref blew the whistle and the Stars kicked off. The team was looking more determined and focused now that we were back up to eleven players, and Hannah, Emily and Jasmin passed the ball around between them in mid-field, not allowing the Belles a look-in. A clever pass from Emily sent Lauren away down the field, and she crossed quickly into the Belles box before any of the defenders could whip the ball away from her. The cross was too high for either Grace or Ruby to connect with and the ball sailed out of play for a goal kick to the Belles.

But just having a go at the Belles goal straight from kick-off had cheered the Stars up, I could see.

'Concentrate, people!' I heard Jacintha yelling at her team. The Belles still looked quite relaxed – well, you would do, wouldn't you, with a three-goal lead? *But if we could just get* ONE *back*, I thought longingly as the Belles goalie took the kick. Then we could really make a fight of it.

But even though I felt OK myself and not too tired, I knew that the other girls had played almost the whole of the first half with just ten players. They were going to be exhausted before the end of the match. The Belles had a lot of fast runners, especially Sienna, and they were known for their lightning movements up and down the pitch. Could we keep up with them right to the very end of the game?

The ball dropped down into mid-field from the goal kick, and Jasmin, Sienna, Sonia Ali and Hannah began fighting for possession. Sonia got the ball first, but Jasmin intercepted her pass to Sienna and side-footed it to Hannah. Alex Lowrie came charging in then and tackled Hannah, sweeping the ball away from her, but I was lurking behind Alex, watching her every move, and I slid in to knock the ball into touch and stop her from making the run forward.

For the first few minutes, it was a real battle in mid-field. But gradually the Belles won the ball and began making their way up the field. Sonia passed to Chloe Parker, who sent it out to Sienna. Immediately Sienna went into her scary sprinter mode and raced off up the wing towards our goal. Jasmin chased after her, a determined look on her face, and all the Belles midfielders followed, knowing this might be the chance for another goal.

I moved across to try and protect Georgie and stop Sienna from getting any closer. I caught Jasmin's eye as she tried to catch up with Sienna, and I knew *exactly* what Jas was thinking. We both knew how selfish Sienna was once she got the ball. She hardly ever passed to anyone. If I timed my tackle just right, Jasmin was right there behind Sienna, waiting to collect the ball. And we could both see a big gap through the middle, now that the Belles midfielders had pushed up…

'Pass, Sienna!' Sonia Ali was screaming.

Sienna ignored her, as I knew she would. She tried to dummy me and cut inside, but I was ready for her because I'd seen her do this several times before when she'd played for the Stars. I hooked the ball away from her, aiming it straight at Jasmin, and it fell almost at her feet. Grinning widely, Jasmin spun round and took off down the pitch.

'Get back!' I heard Jacintha shouting to her midfielders. But Jasmin was flying now! She sent a perfect pass slicing through the gap in the middle of the field to Grace, and she hit it with her first touch to Ruby. Ruby skipped past the player who was marking her and then took a shot at goal as two other Belles defenders rushed to tackle her. The ball hit one of the defenders on the leg and ricocheted into the net, completely wrong-footing the goalie.

Three one! We'd pulled one back!

'Great stuff, guys, but get on with it!' Georgie yelled from our goal. We didn't need telling. We didn't even stop to celebrate. Ruby raced into the net, grabbed the ball and booted it downfield towards the centre circle. Meanwhile, the rest of us rushed back into our positions for kick-off. 'That was a great pass to me, Katy,' Jasmin panted. 'I *knew* Sienna wouldn't let one of her team-mates have the ball!'

'We're a fantastic team, huh?' I slapped Jasmin on the back. 'Let's go for the second goal straight away!'

'Sure thing,' Jasmin agreed. 'I just hope my poor old legs hold out!'

That was my worry, too, I thought, as we kicked off. Getting that goal had given the Stars a real boost, but for how long?

It quickly became obvious that the Belles were now determined to kill the game off once and for all. From the kick-off they surged forward in numbers, and Georgie, Debs, Jo-Jo and me were kept frantically busy as they battered our goal with shot after shot.

'You're playing like a star, Katy!' Georgie shouted at me as I cleared a cross from Sonia Ali safely downfield. It was about the fourth goal attack from the Belles that I'd stopped in the last five minutes.

'I AM a Star!' I shouted back, and then I had to go through the whole routine again as Sienna trapped the ball and came running back towards Georgie's goal. Jo-Jo was nearest to Sienna, but to my dismay, I could see that Jo-Jo was panting hard and looking tired. I dashed over to help her and between us, we got the ball away from Sienna and Jo-Jo passed it to Jasmin. But Jo-Jo's pass wasn't accurate enough and although Jasmin ran for it, she was beaten to the ball by Chloe Parker.

The Belles were on the move again, in the direction of our goal. Chloe had lots of support as she went forward, and as Hattie went to tackle her, Chloe slid the ball over to Sienna. Sienna darted down the wing, and this time I couldn't go over to help Jo-Jo stop her because I was marking Lucy Grimshaw as she hovered menacingly in our penalty area. I couldn't leave Georgie to cope with Tank Girl all on her own!

'PASS, SIENNA!' Jacintha was roaring furiously. 'PASS IT!'

For once, Sienna did as she was told. She sent the ball whizzing over to Jacintha, who tapped it forward to Sonia Ali. Debs tried to tackle Sonia, who easily side-stepped her and then chipped the ball into our box. Lucy rose up to meet it with her head and I jumped with her, but it was no contest because Lucy was at least fifteen centimetres taller than I was. The ball flashed past Georgie's outstretched hand and into the net.

Four one to the Belles.

The whole of the Stars team stopped dead, frozen to the spot wherever they were standing. Even Georgie didn't seem to have the energy to turn and pick the ball up out of the net. She just stood on her goal line staring down the field at the rest of us. The Belles were screaming with delight and hugging each other because they knew they'd got what they wanted – automatic promotion to the top league. Meanwhile, the Stars were stunned, silent and miserable. You can guess who was the most miserable of them all, can't you? I was, of course. Because this was all down to *me*.

The ref was being quite stern with the Belles and telling them to get on with the game. Georgie did finally go and pick the ball out of the net, and she hurled it savagely downfield for us to kick off again.

'That's it, then,' Jasmin said sadly as we got into position. 'There's only a few minutes left to go. We'll never beat them now.'

'We're still in the play-offs,' Grace reminded her.

'Yes, we've still got a chance of promotion,' Hannah agreed. 'As long as—'

'As long as I don't let you down again,' I muttered. I was hurting so much for the girls and for myself, I could hardly bear it. And yet what else could I have done?

'That *wasn't* what I was going to say, Katy,' Hannah replied. 'As long as we stay positive, we've still got a great chance of promotion.'

The Stars kicked off again, but it was all for nothing now. Not only were the rest of the team depressed at losing, they were all beginning to tire badly except me. So it was no real surprise when Sienna scored again about thirty seconds before the end of the game with a fabulous, curling shot after running with the ball at her feet for half the length of the pitch.

And so the match finished 5-1. It was our biggest defeat this season, and it was *so* humiliating. I was gutted, and I could see the other girls felt exactly the same.

The Belles celebrated liked they'd won the World Cup. Without bothering to shake hands with us first, they did a victory lap around the pitch, waving to the crowd. Meanwhile Mrs Gerard, Sienna's mum, produced an expensive-looking digital camera and began taking snaps of the team, but mostly of Sienna. That meant the Stars had to hang around on the pitch, waiting to congratulate the Belles, when all we wanted to do was run off to the changing-room and hide. But then we'd have looked like *really* bad losers.

'I wasn't far off, was I?' Sienna said with a huge grin as she finally bounced over to shake hands with me and Jasmin. She wasn't going to miss a chance to gloat, was she?

'Sorry?' I said blankly. Jasmin was too upset to say anything.

'I predicted six nil to the Belles in the park yesterday evening, remember?' Sienna laughed smugly, showing off her perfect white teeth. 'And now I'm predicting that the Allington Angels will grab the other promotion spot after the play-offs.'

'Why?' I asked bluntly. 'The Angels are third in the table behind us.'

Sienna arched an eyebrow. 'I would have thought it was *obvious*,' she said gleefully. 'You just lost five-one. The Angels will be going into the play-offs too, and they're a good team.'

'Oh, that's right, they beat the Belles, didn't they?' I remarked coolly. 'And yes, you won five one today. But that was because the Stars were a player down for the first half.'

'Only because *you* didn't turn up!' Sienna shot back, really sticking the knife in.

I shrugged, determined not to show that she'd upset me. 'True, but we're going to win the play-offs, so it won't matter anyway.' I must have sounded confident because Sienna got bored with taunting us and walked off towards Jacintha and Lucy.

'Good job, girls,' Sienna said in that faintly patronising tone of hers. 'You were all great.'

Jacintha frowned at her. 'Yes, but we might have got even *more* goals if you didn't hang onto the ball so long! Didn't you hear us yelling at you to pass about a million times?'

Sienna looked annoyed. 'Well, sure I did, but I'm the quickest out of all of you, and I've got a better chance of scoring if I keep the ball as long as I can—'

'Maybe you've forgotten that *I'm* the striker around here, Sienna Gerard!' Lucy responded in a fearsome voice.

Jasmin and I exchanged a faint grin as Lucy, Sienna and Jacintha walked off the pitch, still arguing.

'I'm so glad Sienna's not in our team!' Jasmin exclaimed. 'I'd rather lose out on automatic promotion than play with *her*.'

The rest of the Stars were gathering around us now, and Grace slung her arm across my shoulders.

'Sienna giving you and Jas a hard time?' she asked sympathetically.

'She tried, but Katy handled her brilliantly,' Jasmin replied. 'Sienna's *such* a pain in the butt!'

'Well, I had to do *something*,' I muttered. 'I feel so *bad* about letting you all down—'

'Look, there's no point in going over all this again and again,' Georgie broke in, taking off her baseball cap and shaking out her hair. 'It's over and finished. We've got to put it behind us and get on with concentrating on the play-offs.'

There was a murmur of agreement from the others. I was relieved that no one seemed to hate me for letting them down, especially Georgie, who could be scary where the Stars were concerned! And I knew we might have lost anyway, even if I *had* played the whole game. But I still felt guilty.

Ria came over to us, Lauren limping along beside her.

'It's not the end of the world, girls,' Ria said briskly, looking around at our gloomy faces. Lauren came to stand by me, slipping her arm through mine and giving me a rueful smile. 'Let's look forward to the play-offs, because promotion is still *totally* up for grabs.'

'Sure it is,' Georgie said. 'So let's just get on with it!'

'As we're second in the league, we'll be playing the Turnwood Tigers, who are fifth,' Ria went on.

'And the Allington Angels will be playing the fourth club, the Burnlee Bees. Those matches will be played this Wednesday evening – please, *please* don't tell me some of you can't make it!'

'I wouldn't dare,' Hannah said solemnly. 'Georgie would kill me!'

'Too right,' Georgie agreed.

'I'll be here, I *promise*,' I added.

'Great stuff.' Ria looked relieved. 'And as you know, the winners of those two matches will play off for the remaining promotion place on Saturday.'

'Will we still be training as usual next week, Ria?' asked Ruby.

'No, I want to make sure you all have a good rest,' Ria replied. 'We'll do a shorter session on Tuesday, and then if we win on Wednesday—'

'*When* we win on Wednesday,' Lauren corrected her. Ria grinned.

'That's the spirit!' she said. 'OK, *when* we win on Wednesday, we won't train on Thursday at all, so you'll be fresh for the play-off final on Saturday. Now off you go and get changed, and forget about today. What's done is done.'

Everyone's mood had lightened a bit now, even mine, as we headed for the changing-room.

'No training on Thursday!' Hannah said, looking pleased. 'It's my birthday on Tuesday, but we won't be able to get together because of training and then the game against the Tigers on Wednesday. So do you all want to come round on Thursday for pizza and cake?'

'Pizza and cake? On *Thursday*?' Georgie looked outraged. 'If we get through to the play-off final on Saturday—'

'*WHEN* we get through to the play-off final!' the rest of us said all together.

'OK, OK, *when*,' Georgie repeated. 'Anyway, we need to be super-fit, and not stuffed full of pizza and cake!'

'All right, well, come round to mine for salad and carrot cake, then,' Hannah said, her eyes twinkling. 'Carrot cake's got to be healthy, right?' She turned to me. 'Will you be able to come, Katy?'

'I hope so,' I replied. 'I'll do my best, anyway.'

But I started to get a bit down again as we got changed, although the other girls were chatting away and obviously feeling more upbeat. I was thinking about Hannah's birthday on Thursday. I wasn't even sure I'd be able to afford to buy her a present. I'd never be able to invite the girls to come to a birthday party of mine at *our* flat, would I? Well, I *could*, I suppose, if only I didn't have my stupid pride...

I wish I had more money, I thought glumly as I took the bus home. Mum gave me a bit of pocket money now and again, just so that I could go out with the girls every so often, but I was fed up with not being able to do all the things that they did. If we went to the cinema, even scraping together enough money for a drink was sometimes impossible, never mind a tub of popcorn. The other girls were really generous about sharing with me, although I didn't often accept. But once, just once, I'd love to treat them all. Especially after a day like today when I'd let them down so badly.

But what was the point in brooding about it, I told myself bitterly. That wasn't going to happen...

'Katy's here! Katy's here!'

As I let myself into our flat Milan came galloping to meet me. I picked him up and gave him a huge hug, just as Mum popped her head out of the kitchen to smile at me.

'Did you win, Katy?' Milan asked excitedly.

'Katy, how did it go?' That was my dad calling from the living room.

Instantly I felt just a bit ashamed of myself for being so gloomy earlier. OK, maybe we didn't have much money, but I knew I was lucky to have such a lovely family.

'We lost five one,' I admitted. 'But everyone's really up for the play-offs next week.'

'Oh, poor Katy!' Milan said, and he insisted on giving me another hug, almost squeezing all the breath out of me.

'You look tired, *kochanie*.' Mum came over to take Milan from me. She looked a little guilty. 'I'm so sorry you were late for the match. Go and sit down and I'll make you some lunch. By the way—' she winked at me '—we have a visitor!'

'Is it Magdalina?' I asked.

'No!' Milan giggled, 'Come and see!'

He grabbed my hand and pulled me into the living room. God, I got *such* a shock to see Mrs Jackson sitting there with a cup of tea on the table in front of her! I was even more amazed when Milan rushed into the room behind me, ran over to Mrs J and climbed onto her lap. Mrs Jackson didn't seem to mind a bit, either. In fact, she looked more relaxed than I'd ever seen her before as she settled Milan more comfortably on her knees.

'Mama met Sarah on her way back from work, and invited her in for tea,' Dad explained. *Sarah?!* I stared in shock at Dad, and he flashed me a tiny wink.

'Yes, and I was quite proud of myself for managing to say it in English!' Mum called from the kitchen.

I did a quick calculation in my head. Mum would have got back not long after I left for the match, which meant that Mrs Jackson had been there for almost two hours!

'Are you very disappointed about the game, Katy?' Dad asked sympathetically.

'A bit, because it *was* my fault really that we couldn't give it our best shot, whatever the others say,' I sighed. 'But I'm going to forget about it now and concentrate on the play-offs.'

'I'm sorry to hear that your team lost, Katy,' Mrs Jackson said, and I almost fainted away in surprise! 'Your mum and dad have been telling me all about it.'

'And me!' Milan chimed in, 'I was telling you, too.'

'So you were,' Mrs Jackson agreed, bouncing him up and down on her knees. Milan chuckled with delight. I couldn't believe it. Mrs Jackson seemed like a completely different person. I was actually beginning to *like* her.

'I think I'd better go.' Mrs Jackson glanced at the clock on the wall. 'I have someone coming round to fix my front door very soon.' She glanced at me. 'Then it should close properly, and I won't frighten poor Katy to death again!'

I grinned. 'I frightened you, too,' I said. 'Sorry about that.'

'I could have fixed your door for you, Sarah,' Dad said. 'I'm able to do small jobs now and then when I feel up to it, and it wouldn't have been too difficult. If you need any other carpentry stuff done like putting up shelves or something, just let me know. It would save you paying someone to do it.'

Mrs Jackson looked extremely uncomfortable. 'Oh, there's no need for that,' she muttered stiffly. 'I don't need charity. I like to pay my way.'

I rolled my eyes silently, thinking that it was about time Mrs Jackson learned how to accept help in a more friendly way! Dad was only trying to be nice, after all.

'That's what neighbours are for,' Dad said firmly. I could see that he wasn't going to take no for an answer. 'Back in Poland in our village, everyone looked out for everyone else.'

Mrs Jackson was silent for a moment. 'Well, perhaps I could help *you* out in return by looking after Milan if you ever need a babysitter?' she offered a little shyly.

'Yes, yes, yes!' Milan yelled, beaming all over his face. He gave Mrs Jackson a big hug. 'You don't smell funny like Mrs Zajac does!' he added.

Mrs Jackson and I burst out laughing, and Dad smiled too, although he wagged his finger warningly at Milan. I sneaked a sideways glance at Mrs Jackson as she returned Milan's hug and then put him gently down on the floor. I could hardly believe the change in our neighbour in such a short space of time.

'I think Mrs Jackson is actually a very nice lady underneath it all,' Mum said as she served up lunch a little later. Mrs Jackson had gone home, and we were all around the table eating our sausage soup. 'But the death of her husband was a real shock to her. I don't think she's recovered from it yet, and it's made her very bitter.'

'But if she tried to be more cheerful and a bit less grumpy, she'd be a lot happier!' I pointed out. 'She doesn't seem to want any help from *anyone*.'

'Mrs Jackson is very proud,' Dad replied. 'She's afraid of being pitied and seen as a charity case. She wants to be independent.'

'Well, can't she be independent without being all touchy about it?' I asked.

Mum glanced at Milan, who was apparently busy pulling his bread to bits, and tapped her ears. Dad and I both knew that meant we had to be careful what we said, because Milan was quite often taking everything in, and then he'd repeat it all at the worst possible moment!

'I have a couple of hours' work at the supermarket this afternoon,' Mum said, changing the subject. 'Your dad says he feels up to looking after Milan, Katy, so what are you going to do?'

'Finish off all my homework,' I replied, feeling a sudden surge of energy. That long, deep sleep last night had done me more good than I'd thought. 'And then I'm going to think about how I can help the Stars beat the Turnwood Tigers next Wednesday and get through to the play-off final!'

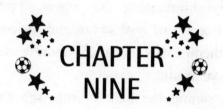

CHAPTER NINE

'Go, go, go!' Georgie yelled at the top of her voice as I swept the ball down the pitch towards Jasmin. 'Get in there, Stars!'

Jasmin booted the ball over to Lauren, who'd completely recovered from her ankle injury, and she took on two Tigers players, beating both of them one after the other. Ruby collected the ball from Lauren and sent a scorching pass directly to Grace in the Tigers' penalty area. Grace brought the ball down neatly and smashed it towards the goal, forcing the Tigers goalie to tip it around the post.

The Stars were really flying already, and it was

only ten minutes into Wednesday night's play-off game, I thought with satisfaction, as I watched Lauren run over to take the corner. At the moment I was staying well back in defence, although later on I'd push forward to attack if we needed to get a winning goal. But at the moment we were completely dominating the Tigers. They'd only had one shot at our goal so far, and Jo-Jo and I had stopped them easily without Georgie needing to make a save at all.

Lauren swung the ball in from the corner and a Tigers defender rose to meet it. She tried to scramble it away, but in the goalmouth confusion, the ball ended up dropping right at Hannah's feet.

'SHOOT!' I heard Georgie roar from behind me. But she groaned as a Tigers defender blocked Hannah's attempt. The ball bounced free and then there was a massive scrum as Grace, Ruby and the other Stars in the box tried to score while the Tigers goalie and defenders desperately tried to get the ball away. It was difficult to see what was happening from the other end of the pitch, but then I saw that Lauren had won the ball. She belted it towards the goal from close range, somehow managing to aim it between the two Tigers defenders who were trying to protect their goalkeeper.

'YES!' Georgie shouted as we all saw the ball fly into the back of the net.

Debs and I exchanged high fives as Lauren was swamped by Grace, Ruby, Hannah, Jasmin and Emily who were all in and around the Tigers penalty area. But the Stars didn't waste long celebrating. Jasmin pelted into the goal and retrieved the ball, charging back to the centre circle to place it ready for the Tigers to kick off. The Tigers were looking a bit glum, but us Stars just wanted to get on with the game immediately, while we were in charge!

Honestly, you'd never have *believed* that we'd lost 5-1 to the Belles on Saturday. Today, every single Stars player was buzzing, including me. I'd had a great weekend and got all my homework done *and* I'd had a rest, too. Mum had been offered another shift at the supermarket on Sunday afternoon, and I'd been all ready to babysit Milan because Dad wasn't feeling so good. But Milan actually begged to go and stay with Mrs Jackson instead! So he went next door, and I curled up on my bed and finished off my homework. I fell asleep, too, in the middle of writing up my science project! But I'd still been able to finish it when I woke up a couple of hours later.

And since I'd caught up on my sleep, I was feeling loads better. We'd only had a short training session on Tuesday too, and that had been a great laugh because it was Hannah's birthday and we'd all brought her cards and presents. Mum had been able to give me a bit of extra pocket money and I'd bought Hannah a funky purse covered with purple and silver beads. She liked it a lot, I think. Then, at the end of the session, Ria had let us all give Hannah the birthday bumps! So all in all, it had been a great week so far, and today was the first match for ages where I really felt I was back to my best.

For the next few minutes the Tigers tried to put a couple of attacks together, but there was nothing we couldn't handle. Georgie gathered up a weak shot from one of the Tigers strikers and then took a goal kick. She hit the ball really hard and it zoomed across the pitch, dropping down into the Tigers' half. Emily went for it, fighting off a Tigers midfielder with help from Jasmin and Hannah. A one-two between Emily and Hannah was broken up by a defender, but Jo-Jo, who'd gone forward a little from the back, was able to win the ball back and send Jasmin away.

Jasmin sent a high ball into the penalty area

towards Grace and Ruby. Grace had her back to the goal and there were Tigers players all around her, so she tried a really spectacular overhead kick! I'd never seen anyone do this while we were playing before – I'd only ever seen it on TV. Grace didn't connect properly with the ball, but she still managed to flick it towards the goal, and it took the Tigers goalie and a defender to scramble it away. And there was Ruby, waiting for the tap-in...

'Two-nil!' Georgie was jumping up and down on her goal-line. Debs and Jo-Jo were hugging me, and I knew then, without a doubt, that the Stars were on our way to the play-offs final on Saturday. We were on a high, and nobody was going to stop us. If we'd been playing the Belles today, we would have mashed them to bits, too, I was sure of it!

Nothing went wrong after that second goal. The Tigers just gave up as the Stars tore them apart with attack after attack. Ria gave us a pep talk at half-time, but as she said herself, we didn't really need it! A fantastic volley from Grace made it 3-0, and then she grabbed a second with an easy header about two minutes later.

Did I say nothing went wrong? Well, that's not *quite* true.

About five minutes before the end, I felt something wasn't quite right with my left foot. I glanced down and to my horror, I saw that the stitching on top of my boot was coming loose. The whole of the upper part was now falling to bits as the stitches unravelled.

I groaned quietly to myself, while still keeping a sharp eye on the ball down at the Tigers' end. My boots *were* ancient, but I'd been praying that they'd keep going until the end of this season. Mum and I had bought them second-hand at a car boot sale just after I'd joined the Stars, and they'd been old and battered even then. My heart dropped as I thought about *somehow* trying to get hold of another pair before the play-off final in three days' time. There was no way I could afford new ones.

But I forgot about my boots when the ref blew the final whistle. What a difference to last Saturday! This time it was *our* turn to celebrate with hugs and high fives, squealing with laughter and fizzing with excitement. Ria ran across the pitch to join us, looking more thrilled than I'd ever seen before.

'Girls, you were brilliant!' she said, her face glowing with delight. 'I'm just waiting for a text from Connie, the Angels manager, to find out who you'll be playing on Saturday, the Angels or the Bees.'

'I hope it's the Bees,' Georgie said. 'The Angels are a tough team to beat.'

There was a murmur of agreement. The Angels had just missed out on promotion last season for the second year running when two of their best players had left the club. They'd be hoping it would be third time lucky for them, I thought. Like Georgie, I'd totally prefer to play the Bees.

Ria's phone beeped. We all waited silently as she read the text that had just arrived.

'The Angels beat the Bees one nil,' Ria said at last.

Georgie pulled a face. 'Oh, well, we'll just have to get on with it, then!'

'If you all play like you did today, you can beat anyone,' Ria assured her, 'Even the Belles. Now off you go and get changed before you get cold.'

The whole team moved off towards the changing-room, still on an enormous high. I hung back a little, squinting down at my left football boot. More stitching had come loose since I'd first noticed it, and I was pretty sure my boots had had it. My dad's really good at patching things up, but I didn't think there'd be anything he could do. I couldn't ask my mum to pay for a new pair, so I'd have to go round the charity shops in town tomorrow after school and see what I could find. It was a real pain.

I was last through the doors into the college, so I stopped just inside and kicked off my boots. I held them tightly against me to hide the damage and then I hurried towards the changing-room. I'd already let the girls down once – I didn't want them to worry about me any more. Besides, I was hopeful the ref might let me play in my trainers if I couldn't get any boots in time. Or maybe Ria could lend me a pair from somewhere. Anyway, I was going to sort it out on my own...

The team was still buzzing when I joined them, but things had calmed down just a little.

'I just got a text from Sienna!' Jasmin said indignantly, waving her phone at me as I came through the door. 'It says congratulations on beating the Tigers, but don't get *too* excited because the Angels are going to thrash the pants off you! Ooh, isn't Sienna just the *worst*?'

'I reckon you should change your phone number, Jas,' Lauren advised her. 'So, how are we going to celebrate getting through to the play-off finals?'

'You're all coming to mine tomorrow now that

Ria's cancelled training, remember?' said Hannah. 'I got some fab prezzies from Mum and Dad on Tuesday, and my grandpa came round for tea, but I haven't done any birthday stuff with my mates, yet.'

'Oh, yes, pizza and cake.' Georgie's eyes lit up. 'I'm so hungry right now, I could eat Jasmin!'

Jasmin giggled and gave her a friendly shove. 'I thought you said we weren't allowed to have pizza and cake before the play-off final?' she reminded Georgie.

'Well, maybe just a *little* bit,' Georgie replied with a grin.

'That's lucky because my mum's made a massive caramel and chocolate sponge!' Hannah told us. 'All round to mine after school, then?' Hannah's gaze switched from Georgie to me. 'Do you think you'll be able to make it, Katy?'

'I'll be there,' I promised, wondering if I'd have time to go into town and look for football boots first. It didn't sound like it, though. I'd have to ask Mum to go for me.

But at that moment I simply had *no* idea just how much a pair of second-hand football boots was going to change my life.

*

'Pizza!' Hannah announced, carrying two large boxes into the Fleetwoods' living room. We were sprawled out on the sofas in there, watching a re-run of a Premier League game – Liverpool vs Chelsea – and Georgie was cracking us up with her cutting comments on the players' ball skills.

'And more pizza,' added Hannah's dad, who was behind her. He was holding another box and also a bag of soft drinks and garlic bread. 'I'll leave you girls to stuff yourselves silly,' Mr Fleetwood went on, depositing the stuff on the dining table at the far end of the large room. 'Just don't eat *so* much that you can't run around on Saturday.'

'That's what *I* keep telling them,' Georgie said. 'We can't go mad when we've got to face the Angels in the play-offs final—' She broke off as Hannah opened one of the boxes, revealing a pizza topped with tuna, sweetcorn and red onions. Georgie's eyes lit up. 'Cool!' she declared, immediately nicking the biggest slice for herself.

The rest of us laughed.

'You're *so* full of it, Georgie!' Lauren teased, opening up one of the other boxes. 'I suppose you're going to have a big slice of cake, too, when you've scoffed all that pizza?'

'Ooh, that reminds me – the cake!' Hannah disappeared off into the kitchen and returned with a huge, lush-looking sponge cake with caramel icing, the two halves of the sponge sandwiched together with chocolate spread. *Happy 13th Birthday, Hannah!* was written in pink icing across it.

'I'm impressed, Hannah,' Grace remarked, biting into a piece of garlic bread. 'Have you been saving this cake up since your birthday on Tuesday?'

'God, no!' Hannah grinned. 'Are you crazy? I had two cakes, actually. This one's just for us.'

Georgie groaned. 'We should be eating salad and fruit,' she complained, reaching for a second slice of pizza.

'Well, I don't care – bring on the junk food!' Jasmin said eagerly. 'I've had to listen to Sienna going on and on all week at school about the Belles getting automatic promotion, and I need cheering-up!'

'This is great, Hannah,' I said, although, as usual, I was secretly aware that I could *never* afford to treat all the girls to a meal like this. 'Thanks for inviting us.'

We'd just started the pizzas when I got a text from Mum, who was on her way home from town. She said she hadn't been able to find any football boots in the charity shops, but she was going to ask around our friends and the people she'd got to know at the supermarket to find out if anyone had a pair in my size that I could borrow. Which was better than nothing, I guess.

And then Grace did something that completely stunned me. We'd mostly finished all the pizzas, and then, while Hannah was cutting the cake, Grace opened her bag and took out a parcel. She pushed it across the table towards me with a nervous smile.

'What's this?' I said, raising my eyebrows. 'Shouldn't you be giving it to Hannah? It's *her* birthday, after all.'

'It's not for Hannah,' Grace replied. She seemed very anxious, although I had no idea why. 'It's for you.'

I was puzzled until I picked the parcel up. Straight away I could tell what was inside, even without unwrapping it.

'What is it?' Jasmin asked curiously.

'Open it, Katy,' Lauren urged. 'We're all dying to see what it is!'

'I already know.' I felt very embarrassed and my voice came out colder than I'd intended it to.

'Well, *we* don't!' Georgie said impatiently. 'Are you going to open it or not?'

I ripped the parcel open then, mainly to buy some time to think about what I was going to say. I couldn't look at Grace as I gazed down at the football boots inside the wrapping paper.

'I noticed one of your boots was falling apart yesterday, Katy,' Grace murmured. She sounded as embarrassed as I was. 'I don't wear this pair any more and I know we have the same size feet, so I thought you might like them. I hope you don't mind me giving them to you in front of the others, but I was hoping they'd help me persuade you to accept them...' Her voice trailed away as she saw the expression on my face.

'Thanks,' I said stiffly, wishing I was a million miles away. It was kind of Grace, but no way was I going to take the boots. 'I *can't* accept them, though.'

'Why not?' Georgie asked bluntly as I offered the boots back to Grace. Grace was looking upset and that made me feel bad, but I was far too proud to back down. 'Are you getting some more for Saturday's game, then?'

'I'm not sure,' I replied, squirming a little at being put on the spot. 'My mum's trying to borrow a pair for me. Then I'll get my own pair for the start of the new season.'

'But you've got a pair now!' Jasmin pointed out, looking totally bewildered. 'Grace has just *given* you some boots!'

'Look, I can't take them, OK?' I mumbled, thrusting the boots back into Grace's arms. 'Now can we just forget about it, please?'

'Well, why don't you just borrow them for Saturday's game, then, Katy?' Lauren asked calmly. 'You said you were going to borrow a pair of boots anyway, so why not Grace's?'

I hesitated. What Lauren was saying *did* make sense.

'OK,' I agreed reluctantly. 'But I'll give them back straight after the game.'

'All right,' Grace agreed, and she put the boots down on the floor by my chair. I still couldn't look at her.

There was silence. I wished now that I'd just taken the boots and shut up about it, but I *couldn't*. Maybe I didn't have much money, but I had my pride. I didn't want the other girls' pity and I didn't want charity either, but now I'd spoilt Hannah's party by being so uptight about everything, and I knew I'd upset Grace, too.

Suddenly the six of us almost jumped out of our

skins as there was a loud – and I mean LOUD – blast of rock music overhead. It was so loud, I swear it set the glass chandelier over the table swinging from side to side!

'What the hell is that?' Georgie asked.

'Don't you mean *who* the hell is that?' Hannah was shrugging and rolling her eyes dramatically. 'It's Olivia, of course. She must have had another row with Dad about Freddie.'

'Freddie's the Unsuitable Boyfriend, right?' Lauren said with a grin.

'Correct,' Hannah sighed. 'Olivia *always* puts her music on full blast when she's in a mood. Mrs Sanderson will be around from next door in a minute to complain.'

'Ooh, that's your weird neighbour, isn't it, Han?' Jasmin remarked. 'The lady who collects garden gnomes?'

'That's her,' Hannah agreed. 'She had thirty-eight in her back garden at the last count. Dad said he's convinced they're starting to breed!'

'Our neighbours are lovely, thank God,' Lauren said.

'How would *you* know?' Georgie scoffed. 'Your garden's about five miles wide, so you don't ever see them!'

Lauren poked her tongue out at Georgie, and I breathed a silent sigh of relief. Things were beginning to get back to normal...

'You've got a funny neighbour, too, haven't you, Katy?' Jasmin said, helping herself to the very last slice of pizza. 'Mrs Johnson, or something like that?'

'*Jasmin!*' Grace hissed warningly. I stared across the table at Jasmin, who instantly turned the brightest red I'd ever seen.

'Well, it's Mrs Jackson, actually,' I replied, frowning. 'And how do you know that, Jas? I don't think I've ever mentioned her to any of you.'

Georgie, Lauren, Grace and Hannah were now exchanging anxious glances with each other. Meanwhile, Jasmin was biting her lip, looking absolutely mortified.

'What's going on?' I asked sharply. 'How do you know about Mrs Jackson?'

None of the girls seemed to know what to say. Then Lauren spoke up.

'Tanya told us,' she said.

'Tanya?' I repeated, still confused. 'What does *your* housekeeper have to do with *my* neighbour?'

Lauren hesitated, looking at the other girls.

'You'd better just tell her,' Georgie said at last.

184

'Tell me WHAT?' I demanded. This was doing my head in.

'Tanya goes to a Polish supermarket sometimes,' Lauren said awkwardly. 'She meets her friend Elizabeta there, and Elizabeta knows Mrs Jackson a bit because they go to the same doctor or something.'

'My mum goes to that supermarket,' I said slowly.

Lauren nodded. 'I think your mum knows Elizabeta, too.'

There was an uncomfortable silence. I remembered my mum mentioning Elizabeta once or twice.

'Does my mum know Tanya?' I asked.

Lauren nodded. 'She's had coffee with Elizabeta and Tanya once, I think.'

'So I suppose Tanya came back and repeated all the things my mum told her?' My voice was shaking as it all finally began to sink in. 'I suppose now you know *everything* about my dad's illness and the shabby old flat where we live and why my mum has to work so hard and our neighbour Mrs Jackson, and you've been talking about it behind my back for ages!'

'Katy, that's not how it is at all,' Grace said firmly. 'Tanya *did* tell Lauren everything, but she didn't realise until after she'd got home that it was probably *your* mum she'd met in the supermarket.'

'Tanya didn't know that you'd kept all this quiet from us, Katy,' Lauren added. 'She was very upset when she found out, so we agreed it was best not to say anything to you. And the others thought so, too—'

Humiliated and angry, I jumped to my feet.

'So *that's* why you were all so nice to me when I was missing training and being late for everything!' I exclaimed. 'Because you felt sorry for me!'

'Well, it's not a crime, is it?' Georgie pointed out reasonably enough, but I wasn't in the mood to listen. 'We just wanted to help you out, Katy—'

'I don't *need* help, and I don't like you all talking about me behind my back!' I snapped furiously. Everything was falling into place now, like that text from Lauren suddenly cancelling the trip the girls had planned to the leisure centre – probably because Tanya had told them all about our money difficulties with Mum's wages being cut. I was *boiling* with fury.

'What other choice did we have?' asked Hannah. 'You're our friend, Katy, and we love you to bits. But you *never* let us do anything for you—'

I was about to open my mouth to say that I didn't *want* them to do anything for me; that I had my pride and I was very independent and I didn't want charity and I didn't need pity... But suddenly I could hear Mrs Jackson saying the very same words to me and Dad a few weeks ago. And what had I thought to myself about Mrs Jackson?

She was letting her stupid pride get in the way of enjoying her life...

She ought to be nicer to people who were trying to help her...

I *wasn't* like Mrs Jackson. Was I?

Suddenly I had to get away.

I slid out of my seat, grabbed my bag and ran to the front door, even though the others called me back.

It was only when I was halfway home that I realised I'd left the football boots behind.

CHAPTER
TEN

Half an hour later I was still upset when I reached our garden gate. So I stopped and tried to calm myself down before I went up to the flat. Mum and Dad would notice straight away that something was wrong, and I didn't want to have to explain everything to them.

Already I was feeling like a right idiot, running out on the girls like that. But I really *was* angry that they'd known everything about my whole life for the last couple of weeks, and never said a word. The thought of them discussing me and all my problems without me knowing about it upset me like nothing else.

It was cold just standing there by the gate, so I decided to go for a walk to calm down a little more before I went home. But as I turned to leave, someone called my name.

'Katy?'

I recognised the voice. I looked around and saw Mrs Jackson standing on her doorstep.

'Are you all right, Katy?' she called hesitantly.

I opened my mouth to reply that I was fine, but all of a sudden I felt like I was going to burst into tears right there and then. Horrified, I stared at Mrs Jackson, biting my lip and blinking hard to stop myself crying.

'Come inside.' Mrs Jackson beckoned to me, opening the door wider. 'It's freezing out here.'

I didn't really want to, but I realised that I didn't have a lot of choice. I couldn't go home in this state and upset everyone. And Mrs J was right – it *was* freezing. Reluctantly I went down her front path and into the house.

Mrs Jackson didn't say a word as she led me along the hall and into her kitchen. I looked around curiously as I unwound my scarf from my neck. The kitchen reminded me of my gran's, back home in Poland. There was a black cooking range which warmed the room, and Mrs Jackson had obviously been baking because there was a rack of scones cooling on the worktop. There was even a wooden rocking-chair by the range that reminded me of one my gran had. I tried desperately not to let my feelings run away with me, but I couldn't stop my eyes filling with tears.

'Oh dear!' Mrs Jackson exclaimed, looking a little anxious. She was probably already regretting inviting me in. 'Sit down, Katy, and I'll put the kettle on.'

I sat down in the rocking-chair and began to rock gently to and fro which calmed me a little.

'I was just waiting at the window watching out for my son, when I spotted you,' Mrs Jackson explained as the kettle boiled. 'Adrian, Colette and my grandchildren are popping over to visit me this evening.'

'Oh, I'm in the way, then!' I exclaimed, horrified. 'I'd better go—'

'No, please stay, Katy,' Mrs Jackson said quickly. 'They won't be here for a little while yet. I'm just so excited about seeing them, I was looking out for them before they were due.' She gave an embarrassed little laugh. 'So how was your friend's birthday party?'

I stared at her in surprise.

'Milan told me.' Mrs Jackson smiled at me. 'He tells me lots of things.'

Oh, bum! I thought, trying not to look nervous. Milan had such a big mouth!

'Well, we were having a great time until I went and spoilt it all,' I said with a sigh.

'How?' Mrs Jackson asked.

I didn't have any intention of telling Mrs J the whole story, so I just told her the bit about Grace wanting to give me the boots and how I couldn't accept them. But then Mrs Jackson handed me a cup of tea and started asking me questions, and I couldn't stop it all flooding out. How my family were so poor compared to the other girls' parents, how I never had enough money to do all the stuff the girls did and how I was so proud and as prickly as a hedgehog if ever any of the girls wanted to give me anything or help me out. I didn't want charity and I hated being pitied for not having any money. And even while I was speaking, I knew that what I'd thought earlier was true – Mrs Jackson and I *were* like each other! And I'd been so annoyed about her not accepting kindnesses from other people. I hadn't realised until now that I was doing exactly the same thing...

I could see from Mrs Jackson's face that her thoughts were mirroring mine. And judging from her expression, she was feeling just as bad about it as I was myself.

'Don't be so hard on yourself, Katy,' Mrs Jackson said with a rueful smile. 'I'm a *lot* older than you, and I've made exactly the same mistakes. I should know better!' She sighed. 'My husband died very suddenly and *very* unexpectedly, and it knocked me for six. I was just *obsessive* about being determined to cope on my own and not be a burden to my family.'

'That's how I feel about my friends,' I said.

'And has that made you happy?' Mrs Jackson asked.

'No.' It was my turn to sigh deeply now. 'All it's done is make my life more difficult.'

'There's nothing wrong with wanting to be independent and stand on our own two feet,' Mrs Jackson said thoughtfully. I could tell she was talking to herself, as well as to me. 'But if people love and care for you, and you're having a hard time, then naturally they want to help. And by turning them down, you make them feel bad...'

A picture of Grace's distressed face when I'd refused the football boots popped into my head.

Now I felt *really* guilty. It must have taken Grace a lot of courage to give me the boots, knowing the way I was likely to react.

'But it's different for you,' I said. 'Like, you know when my dad offered to do some jobs for you?'

Mrs Jackson nodded. 'Yes, I'm afraid I was a little ungracious about it at the time,' she admitted, turning pink with embarrassment.

'But *you* offered to look after Milan in return, and that helped us out *loads*,' I went on. 'And he loves coming to see you.'

There was actually a twinkle in Mrs Jackson's eyes. 'Because I don't smell funny like Mrs Zajac?'

'That helps!' I smiled at her. 'But the reason why I sometimes feel so awkward with my friends is because *I* can't treat them to anything the way they treat *me*. I've been to their houses lots of times and to their birthday parties and whatever, and *I'd* never be able to afford to do anything like that for them. I've never even invited them to our flat because it's so small.'

Mrs Jackson sipped her tea. 'Have your friends ever made any comments to you about all this?'

'Of course not!' I exclaimed in horror. 'They're way too nice to do *that*.'

'So it's *you* who thinks all these things and not the other girls, then?' Mrs Jackson pointed out. 'You know, Katy, maybe they don't want anything in return from you – except your friendship. Maybe that's enough for them?'

I stared at Mrs Jackson in amazement. I'd never thought of it that way before.

'Thank you,' I said, putting my empty cup down on the table. I was actually beginning to feel a little better, thanks to Mrs Jackson. It had been good to talk things through with someone who understood. 'I'd better go now before your family gets here.'

'Your dad said to bring them up to your flat to meet you all.' Mrs Jackson escorted me to the front door. 'So I'll see you later, as long as your dad feels up to it.'

'Oh, Dad loves meeting new people,' I replied. 'See you later, then. And thanks again.'

Mrs Jackson looked pleased as she waved me goodbye. *People like to help and to feel needed,* I thought as I went home. But had my stubborn attitude driven all my friends away for good?

I suddenly thought how much Dad, Mum and Milan would enjoy meeting Jasmin, Grace, Hannah, Lauren and Georgie. I talked about them a lot at home, and Milan could even recite all their names! And yet neither Mum nor Dad had ever asked me why I hadn't invited the girls to visit us. Did they guess that I didn't want the girls to see where I lived? Did Mum and Dad think I was ashamed of them? That made me feel so guilty, I couldn't bear it.

'Enough, Katy!' I told myself silently. 'It's about time you put a stop to this, once and for all.'

I fumbled in my pockets for my front-door key and my phone. Then I let myself into the house and keyed in a text as I slowly climbed the stairs.

Sorry, I'm such an idiot : (Can we meet & talk??? K x

Then I sent it to all the girls.

'Oh, I wasn't expecting you back yet, Katy,' Mum called from the kitchen as I opened the door of the flat. 'Did you have a good time at Hannah's?'

'Yes, thanks,' I called back. It seemed the easiest thing to say, even though it was a bit of a fib. I was hoping that I'd get a text back from at least *one* of the girls really quickly so that I could make everything all right again. But I checked my phone as I went into the living room, and there was nothing. Not a single text.

'Are you OK, *kochanie*?' Dad asked. He was doing a dinosaur jigsaw with Milan on the coffee table. 'You look a little worried.'

'Oh no, I'm fine,' I replied breezily. But secretly I was panicking. What if Hannah, Lauren, Grace, Georgie and Lauren had had enough of me? I *couldn't* lose the best and most loyal friends I'd ever had.

'Mrs Jackson said you'd invited her to bring her family over when they visit tonight,' I remarked to Dad.

He looked surprised. 'That's true, Katy, but when did *you* see Sarah?'

'Oh, she popped out to say hello to me when I arrived home just now,' I answered quickly. Which was true, wasn't it?

'Katy, could you come and give me a hand?' Mum called. I went out to the kitchen, checking my phone again on the way. Still nothing.

'I bought some pastries at the supermarket for Mrs Jackson and her family when they come over. Could you put them in the oven to warm up, please?' Mum handed me a stack of boxes. There were enough pastries there to feed the whole street! 'I wanted to do some baking today, but I didn't have time,' Mum went on, filling up the kettle. 'Mr Kowalski offered me another shift at the supermarket this afternoon, and then I went to town afterwards to look for some football boots for you. I haven't had any luck finding a pair for you to borrow, though.'

'Don't worry about it, Mama,' I said, hoping against hope that I could sort things out with the girls and maybe still use Grace's boots. But why hadn't any of them replied to my message?

I took my phone out to check it again, and at that moment the doorbell rang.

'That will be Mrs Jackson and her family,' Mum guessed.

'I'll go,' I said. I gave the pastries back to Mum and hurried downstairs. But when I opened the door, expecting to see Mrs Jackson and her son, daughter-in-law and grandchildren, I got a real shock.

Grace, Hannah, Georgie, Lauren and Jasmin were standing outside.

CHAPTER ELEVEN

'What are *you* doing here?' I gasped. I was staring at the girls like my eyes were about to pop out of my head. I couldn't believe they were right here on the doorstep!

'Tanya told us your address and Hannah's dad gave us a lift,' Georgie said, a determined look on her face. 'We want to get all this sorted out before the play-off final, Katy.'

'Yes, and I've risked *serious* injury by coming to see you, Katy,' Jasmin squeaked indignantly. 'There were four of us crushed into the back seat of Mr Fleetwood's car, and Georgie was almost sitting on top of me! So you've *got* to be nice to us now!'

Even though Grace, Hannah and Lauren were smiling at me, I could see that their eyes were anxious. They were all wondering how I was going to react, and I knew that whatever I did now would make or break our friendship for ever.

'Oh, God, I'm *so* glad to see you!' I exclaimed, throwing my arms around Hannah, who was nearest. 'Thank you for coming.'

The girls looked totally relieved.

'We got your texts when we were already on our way here,' Lauren explained. 'Tanya told us your address. We weren't quite sure what you were going to do if we just turned up, but hey, we did it anyway!'

'And I'm glad you did,' I replied, clinging onto Hannah's arm. 'Come upstairs and meet my family.'

'Really?' Hannah's face lit up. She didn't seem to be noticing the battered old front door, the weed-filled front garden or the tatty carpet in the hall behind me. 'We'd love to.' She held up the carrier bag she was holding. 'And we have cake!'

'Hannah brought her birthday cake along,' Grace explained, 'seeing as we didn't get a chance to eat it.'

I smiled at her.

'Sorry,' I said. 'I was an idiot about the boots. It was lovely of you to think of me—'

'Forget it, Katy.' Grace gave me a hug.

'Ooh, I love it when we all make up,' Jasmin sighed happily.

'Can we stop with the hugging now?' Georgie asked. 'There's a large piece of cake inside that bag that's calling my name, and I have to eat it – *now*!'

'Come in.' I held the door open wider so that the girls could troop inside. Then I led them up the stairs.

'Who lives there, Katy?' Lauren asked, pointing at the ground-floor door.

'Some student nurses,' I replied. 'They can be a bit noisy sometimes, but they're OK. One of them called an ambulance for my dad when he was ill.'

'What's wrong with him?' Jasmin asked a little warily. 'You never really said, Katy.'

'Well, he has ME,' I explained. 'You probably don't know what it is—'

'Oh, *I* do,' Georgie broke in. 'It's horrible. One of my aunts has it. She's exhausted the whole time, and she catches all sorts of infections.'

'Yes, I remember you telling me about it once, Georgie,' said Grace.

I could hardly get my head around all this. I'd *never* thought that the girls would understand about my dad's illness – and here was Georgie saying very calmly that she knew all about it because her aunt was the same! She'd have helped me to explain it to the other girls, if only I hadn't been so uptight about it all. I truly was a really BIG idiot...

'Mind the hole in the carpet,' I told them at the top of the stairs. 'I'd better just warn everyone you're coming.' I stuck my head around the flat door and yelled 'Mum, Dad, my friends from football are here. Is it OK if they come in?'

Mum hurried out of the kitchen, wiping her hands on a towel, her face alight with a welcoming smile.

'Of course, of course, bring them in!' she said in Polish, and then in English, 'Hello, hello.'

'Come in, girls,' Dad was calling from the living room. 'Milan and I are longing to meet you.'

I took the girls into the living room. Milan came over all shy when he saw them, and he climbed into Dad's arms, hiding his face against Dad's shoulder.

'It's great to see you, girls,' Dad said, looking brighter than he'd done all day. 'Katy talks about you all the time.'

'Does she?' Lauren asked. 'All good stuff, I hope!'

'She says that you're the best friends she's ever had,' Milan muttered shyly, taking a quick peek at them.

'Oh, you must be Milan!' Jasmin exclaimed. She went over and sat down on the sofa next to Dad. 'This is a fab dinosaur jigsaw puzzle. Are you doing it all by yourself?'

Milan nodded solemnly. 'Dad tries to help me, but he gets it all wrong!'

We all laughed. Mum looked puzzled, so I quickly translated Milan's comment into Polish for her.

'I bet you can't guess what *my* name is,' Jasmin said to Milan.

Milan squinted at her for a moment. 'I think you're Jasmin,' he said triumphantly. The surprised look on Jasmin's face made us all howl with laughter once more.

'How do you know *that*?' Jasmin demanded with a grin.

'Because Katy said you had black hair and you wore funny clothes!' Milan explained. And he pointed at Jasmin's bright pink knitted hat with the multi-coloured ribbons hanging off the back of it.

'*Milan!*' said Dad, but Jasmin was giggling away, not offended in the least.

'Do you know *all* our names?' asked Georgie. So Milan had a go at naming each one of the girls. He didn't do too badly except he got Lauren and Grace mixed up!

'I'll get some juice and pastries for everybody,' Mum told me, heading off to the kitchen.

By now Milan and Jasmin were the best of friends and she started helping him with his jigsaw. My dad was asking Lauren, Georgie, Hannah and Grace all about themselves and about the Stars, so I left them chatting and slipped away to give Mum a hand.

'It's great to meet your friends at last, Katy,' Mum said casually as she took the juice out of the fridge. 'They seem like lovely girls.'

'Yes,' I replied proudly. 'They are.' *And it had taken me a long time to realise just how wonderful my friends really were.*

'Can we help?' asked Grace. She and Hannah had come to stand in the kitchen doorway.

'Sorry, there's not much room in here,' I said apologetically.

'Oh, it's fine,' Hannah replied. She and Grace squeezed into the kitchen and began to take the slices of birthday cake out of the tin they were packed in. Behind me I could hear Milan and Jasmin discussing which piece of the jigsaw went where. I could also hear Georgie and Lauren making my dad laugh as they described some of the matches we'd played this season. Everything seemed so *right* all of a sudden.

Another ring at the doorbell five minutes later, and Mrs Jackson and her family arrived just in time for juice, coffee and cake. We had hardly any chairs left, but Jasmin, Georgie and Lauren were happy to perch on the floor, making room for Mrs Jackson, her son Adrian and his wife Colette to sit down. Adrian was a tall, thin man with round silver glasses, and his wife was small and slight with gorgeous flame-red curls. The kids, Edward and Stella, were both *so* cute. I think Milan fell in love with Stella, who was the same age as him, straight away – she was like a little doll with porcelain-pale skin and the same red hair as her mum. She and Edward were a bit shy at first, but they took to Jasmin instantly and within a few minutes they too were helping eagerly with the dinosaur jigsaw.

Suddenly our shabby little flat was full of people and we didn't really have enough room for them, but you know what? It didn't matter a *bit*. The place was full of chatter and laughter and the smell of hot coffee and pastries warm from the oven, and no one seemed to care that our flat was so small and that our sofa and chairs didn't match and that our curtains had seen better days.

Dad was enjoying himself so much, chatting to Mrs Jackson, Adrian, Colette and the girls. But I felt a bit sorry for Mum. Although she was loving having everyone there, she couldn't understand much of what was going on, so every so often I translated bits of what everyone was saying into Polish for her.

'I'll have to leave for work now, Katy,' Mum told me eventually. 'I'm late already! It's been *so* nice having everyone to visit, but I *wish* I could speak more English.' She heaved a sigh. 'I feel like I'm missing out...'

Mrs Jackson's daughter-in-law, Colette, was watching Mum and I talking. She leaned over and tapped my arm.

'Your mum doesn't speak English, Katy?' Colette asked.

I shook my head. 'I think she'd like to learn, but we couldn't afford to pay for lessons,' I replied.

'Well, I work at a community centre not far from

here,' Colette told me. 'We have lots of stuff going on, and among other things, we offer free English lessons to people who've moved to the UK.'

'Really?' I exclaimed. Mum was frowning, trying to follow what we were saying, so quickly I explained in Polish. When she understood, she looked thrilled.

'That would be wonderful!' Mum said. 'It would be tough to fit it in around work, but I'd really *love* to do it.'

'We also run quite a few schemes to help people who aren't very mobile, for whatever reason, like your dad,' Colette went on. 'We have a minibus as well as volunteers who offer lifts, and things like that. And we can also help you check that you're getting all the help you're entitled to from the government, if you like?'

When I translated all this for Mum, she looked so happy, I thought she was going to cry. Which made *me* want to cry. Wasn't it amazing how opening up our lives to everyone was helping *us* so much, too?

Milan was now showing Georgie, Edward, Stella and Jasmin his collection of plastic dinosaurs that Mum and I had bought at a car boot sale.

'You know, my brothers were really into dinosaurs

when they were a bit younger, Milan,' Georgie remarked, examining a battered old model of a tyrannosaurus rex. 'We've got loads of their dino stuff knocking around at home. Shall I bring it over for you?'

Milan looked incredibly excited. 'Yes, please!' he shouted. 'Thank you, Georgie.'

Suddenly Georgie glanced at me anxiously, wondering if she'd gone and put her foot in it. I smiled at her and mouthed, *It's fine!* Georgie looked relieved and grinned widely at me.

Then I turned to Grace, who was sitting near me.

'It was wonderful of you to offer me those boots, Grace,' I said in a low voice. 'And I'd love to have them, if you still want me to.'

Grace smiled. She opened her bag and handed me the boots, which were still wrapped in paper. 'Of course I want you to have them, Katy,' she said. 'You never know, they might help you to become a brilliant player, just like me!'

I burst out laughing. Taking the boots didn't seem like charity to me, now. I just knew that I was lucky to have the most understanding friends in the whole world.

CHAPTER TWELVE

It was a very special day for me and for the Stars. It was Saturday, the day of the play-off final between us and the Allington Angels. It was breezy, but the sky was blue and the sun kept peeping out through the clouds every so often. It was a perfect day for football, I thought, as the ref told us to take up our positions for the start of the game.

But the reason today was extra-special for me was because my mum, dad and Milan were here to see me play for the very first time! Dad had mentioned to Adrian on Thursday that he'd never been to one of my football matches. Adrian had then offered to pick up me, Dad and Milan – and Mrs Jackson, who also wanted to come! – in his people carrier, and bring us to the game. Colette and the kids had come too, so for once I had loads of people supporting me! Colette had even managed to borrow a wheelchair from the community centre so that Dad didn't have to walk very far. Mum had come too, straight after she finished work, on the bus.

'That's my sister,' I heard Milan telling Ria proudly as I jogged down the pitch with Georgie towards our end. I'd introduced Ria to my family a few minutes before, and now she was standing with them to watch the game.

'I know, and she's a very good player, too,' Ria said, smiling at him.

'God, I'm nervous!' Georgie moaned to me as she headed towards her goal. 'Do you think the Angels are nervous as well?'

'Of course they are,' I said. 'They've missed out on promotion a couple of times already, haven't they?'

Georgie nodded. 'They'll be going for it today.'

'And so will *we*,' I reminded her. I glanced around the pitch at the other Stars. Jasmin was jigging about from one foot to the other, fiddling with her hair, Ruby looked petrified, Lauren was biting her lip and Grace was very pale. It was a bit worrying, but then, I was feeling almost sick with tension myself. I *so* wanted to do well in front of my family. We'd all be OK once the game got started, I hoped.

The ref blew his whistle and the game kicked off. Ria had warned us not to go all out to grab an early goal, which would mean leaving gaps at the back for the Angels to take advantage of. Instead she'd told us to take our time and settle in for the first few minutes. It was obvious that the Angels manager had told *them* exactly the same thing because to start with, no one on either team seemed to want to do anything other than pass the ball around safely in midfield. It took me a little while to get used to Milan cheering loudly every time I touched the ball, too!

Then the Angels started getting bolder. They had a really good striker, Elena Rivers, who was very quiet for the first ten minutes, but gradually she started getting into the match. A pass from one of the Angels midfielders sent her clear of our defence, and though I rushed across to try and block her shot, Elena managed to thump it towards the goal. Luckily Georgie was there to gather it safely up into her arms. But a few minutes later, Elena was back again, collecting a cross from Marie-Jayne Cooper (the girl who'd slipped on the banana skin last year and broken her leg!) and sending a shot whistling past the post.

'We need to step up a gear!' Georgie panted as she ran back with the ball to take the goal kick.

Georgie was right, and she started us off by whacking the ball right into the Angels' half. Jasmin trapped the ball and brought it down, struggling with Marie-Jayne Cooper, who rushed over to try to claim it for the Angels. Jasmin just about managed to keep the ball away from Marie-Jayne and send Hannah away with it in the direction of the Angels goal. From Hannah, the ball went spinning over to Lauren, then to Ruby and on to Grace, who was clear in the box. It looked like a simple chance for Grace to score, but she mis-hit the ball and it rolled harmlessly out of play for a goal kick to the Angels.

The Stars had got some confidence going now, though, and having stopped a weak Angels attack, we surged forward again. I didn't dare go too far up the field yet because the Angels were very quick on the break and I didn't want to leave Georgie without any back-up. But I pushed up a little so I could watch what was going on. I kept a sharp eye on

Elena Rivers, though, who was lurking around the centre circle with me!

Emily and Lauren were knocking the ball around between them, not allowing the Angels to have it but not getting very far forward, either. Then Emily spotted Jasmin making a run into a space the Angels had left wide open. She chipped the ball over to her, and I held my breath as Jasmin raced into the box. She was in a *great* position to score!

'Shoot, Jas!' I heard Georgie yelling behind me.

Jasmin drove in a shot at goal, but like Grace's before her, it flew past the post. We didn't have time to do or say anything, though, because the Angels goalkeeper took the goal kick really quickly, leaving us all flustered and out of position.

'Get back to help out!' I yelled at Jasmin, Hannah, Lauren and Emily as Marie-Jayne Cooper went flying up the field again, the ball at her feet. She'd already beaten Jo-Jo, and she was looking ahead to pick out Elena Rivers in the box.

The ball came in and I leapt up and headed it out. It landed on the grass just outside the box. Jasmin was closest, but as she went to clear it, she slipped on a patch of mud and fell over. Instantly Elena Rivers hooked the ball away and hit a shot on the turn. Georgie didn't even see it coming until it had whizzed past her into the net.

One-nil to the Angels.

It wasn't the end of the world because we had loads of time left to catch up, but it was a shock, nevertheless. We glanced at each other in dismay as the Angels celebrated gleefully.

'Come on, Stars!' Georgie shouted, kicking the ball downfield to the centre circle. 'We're going to get one back before half-time!'

But as the first half went on, I began to notice that Grace wasn't playing very well. She seemed to be slow running for the ball, and whenever I got a glimpse of her, she looked even paler than when we'd first started the game. What was the matter with her? I wondered.

'Is Grace ill?' Debs asked me as we waited for the Angels to take a throw-in. 'She doesn't look her normal self today.'

'No, she doesn't,' I agreed. Then a few minutes before half-time, Grace fluffed a pass to Ruby that might have led to an equaliser, and I could see from the looks on the others' faces that they too had realised something wasn't quite right.

'Sorry, guys,' Grace said unhappily as we trooped

off at half-time, the score still 1-0. 'Sorry, Ria. I started feeling ill just before the game began. I've got a horrible headache and a sore throat, and I think I'm getting a cold.'

'Do you want to come off the field?' Ria began.

'God, no!' Grace looked horrified. Hattie Richards couldn't make it today, so we didn't have a sub. 'I'll be OK.'

'Girls, I think we're going to have to take a few more chances in the second half,' Ria said thoughtfully. 'Katy—' she turned to me '—I think it's time for you to push forward a little more. The Angels won't be expecting that. We need your height in the Angels box to get a quick goal as soon as we can into the second half.'

I nodded. 'Let's go for it!' I said. I glanced over at my parents and Milan, who were waving at me. I wanted to win the match for *them*, too, as well as for the Stars.

The second half began, and I did as Ria had told me. Leaving Jo-Jo, Alicia and Debs to cover Georgie, I began pushing deeper into the Angels' half, taking the ball further and further each time. This meant that the midfield players could also push forward, although Emily stayed back a little to help out Alicia, Debs and Jo-Jo.

For five or ten minutes we battered the Angels' goals with shots and crosses from all angles. Then I drifted out onto the wing and lobbed a high ball into the Angels box, which was full of Stars players. I was aiming for Hannah, who was one of the tallest girls in there.

Hannah leapt for the ball, but I groaned in dismay as it flew over her, just grazing the top of her head and not allowing her to get a shot in. But then the ball dropped down right in front of Jasmin.

'I've got it!' Jasmin squealed excitedly. She was so close to the goal, she couldn't miss. Could she?

No, she couldn't! Jasmin gave the ball a thump with her right foot and it zoomed over the line and into the goal in a black and white blur.

One all! At last!

This time it was the Angels' turn to look gutted as the Stars celebrated noisily. We soon stopped hugging and high-fiving each other, though, when we spotted Ria tapping her watch. We all knew what she was saying. *You need to finish this game off now, otherwise you'll be playing extra time…*

'We can do this!' I told the others. 'Let's go for another goal while the Angels are looking so depressed.'

Everyone nodded, even Grace, who was looking more ill than she had at half-time. So as soon as the Angels kicked off, the Stars were hustling for the ball, going for every challenge and generally making a nuisance of themselves.

But the Angels were a great team, and after we'd had three or four shots at their goal – and Grace had hit the crossbar – they soon pulled themselves together and came storming back. Then it was end-to-end stuff. Elena Rivers had two shots that hit the posts, and a volley from Lauren at the other end was cleared off the line by an Angels defender. Marie-Jayne's free kick soared over Georgie's head and almost beat her, but somehow Georgie managed to bend backwards and fingertip it over the bar. It was a brilliant save and it kept us in the game. Then we went close ourselves with attempts by Ruby and Jasmin.

Time was ticking away now. Ria was glancing anxiously at her watch every few seconds, and we all knew there was very little time left to go.

I was determined that the game *wasn't* going to go into extra time! Collecting the ball from Georgie, I made a run down the pitch, passing the ball to Alicia, Emily and Jasmin along the way. I got the ball back from Jasmin deep in the Angels' half, just as Hannah went shooting up the wing on my right. I hung onto the ball, fighting off the Angels defenders who tried to rob me, until I could see Hannah approaching the penalty area. And then I passed to her.

Hannah received the ball just inside the box and tried to take it around the Angels defender who was stalking her. Looking panicked, the defender stuck out her leg, with absolutely no chance of getting the ball, and sent Hannah flying.

Immediately the ref blew his whistle and pointed to the spot.

PENALTY!

None of us could quite believe what was happening. With only a few minutes to go, this penalty could take us up into the top league! Quickly all the Stars huddled together to decide who was going to take it.

'Oh, God!' Lauren breathed. She was as white as a sheet. 'Grace, can you do this?'

Grace was looking very nervous. 'I don't know,' she confessed. 'I'm feeling so ill.'

'Ruby, then?' Georgie turned to look at our other striker, but Ruby was just as pale as Lauren.

'What if I miss?' Ruby blurted out 'You'll all hate me!'

'No, we won't,' Jo-Jo assured her, but Ruby didn't look at all convinced.

'I bet I'll trip over my shoelace or something if I do it,' Jasmin muttered anxiously.

I took a deep breath. 'I'll take the penalty,' I said.

The whole team turned to stare at me.

'Really?' Hannah asked.

I nodded.

'You can do it, Katy,' Georgie said, patting me on the back. But I could see the tension in her face.

The ref was looking impatient now so I took the ball and placed it on the penalty spot. I had just realised that *this* was the way I could repay my friends for all their kindness to me over the last year or two. By scoring the goal that would win us promotion and take us up to the top league.

I didn't glance over at my parents and Milan, but I knew their eyes would be fixed on me, silently willing me to succeed. But the next second I forgot there was anyone else in the world except me and the Angels goalie.

I took a run-up to the ball. I wanted to hit it as hard as I could, but it had to be placed properly.

I didn't want to sky it.

My right foot connected with the ball. It flew off the ground and although the Angels goalkeeper went the right way, my shot was too hard and too high into the net for her to make the save.

'GOAL!' I heard the Stars yelling above the applause of the crowd. And the next moment I was swamped with hugs by the other girls, their faces full of delight and relief. The ref didn't allow us to celebrate for long, though. He hustled us back to the centre circle, but no sooner had the Angels kicked off again, than the full-time whistle blew. We shook hands with the disappointed Angels, and then we just went *mad*.

'We did it!' Jasmin screamed joyfully, dancing crazily around the pitch with Lauren, Ruby and Jo-Jo. 'We got promotion! Ooh, wait till I tell Sienna!'

'League One, here we come!' Hannah, Alicia, and Emily were chanting. They had their arms around each other and were jumping up and down without stopping.

'OK, so next season we have to be *top* of the top league, guys!' Georgie declared. Despite saying she didn't like hugs, she was now hugging everyone close to her!

'You were brilliant, Katy.' Grace slapped me on the back. 'Thank you for taking that penalty. I just didn't feel up to it.'

'Oh, but I only scored because I was wearing your boots!' I said with a grin, and Grace laughed.

'OK, team celebration!' Georgie ordered.

'What, even more hugs?' asked Lauren.

Georgie shook her head. 'Nah, enough with the hugs!' she said, linking hands with me and Hannah. 'Come on, everyone, hold hands!'

We did as Georgie said, and then all eleven of us ran across the pitch in one long line. When we reached the other side, we all dived forward onto the grass and rolled around there, shrieking with laughter as our parents took a whole load of photos.

And I knew that there was nowhere else I'd rather be than right here, right now, with all my friends and family around me as we celebrated promotion together.

My life might not be perfect, but I loved it!

About the Author

Narinder Dhami lives in Cambridge with her husband Robert and their three cats, but was originally born in Wolverhampton. Her dad came over from India in 1954, and met and married her mum, who is English. Narinder always wanted to write, but after university taught in London for ten years before becoming a writer.

For the last thirteen years Narinder has been a full-time author. She has written over 100 children's books, as well as many short stories and articles for children's magazines. *Katy's Real Life* is the sixth book in The Beautiful Game series.

Since her childhood, Narinder has been a huge football fan.

A message from the England Women's Captain
FAYE WHITE

With over 1.5 million playing the game, girls' and women's football is now the number one female sport. I have played for Arsenal and England ladies since I was sixteen. I grew up kicking a ball around – in the playground, at school, or in my back garden. I was the only girl playing amongst boys, but I never let that stop me, and I joined my first club at thirteen.

For me, playing football has always been about passion and enjoyment. It's a great way to challenge myself, be active, gain self–confidence, and learn about teamwork.

I have gone on to captain and play for England seventy times, and achieved my dream of playing in a World Cup (China 2007). I've won over twenty-five honours for Arsenal, including the treble, and the Women's UEFA Cup.

Do you love football as much as me?

Then maybe, just maybe, you can follow in my shoes... Practice, be passionate and strive for your dream. Enjoy!

Find out more about Faye and girls' football at...

www.faye-white.co.uk   www.thefa.com/womens
www.arsenal.com/ladies   www.fairgamemagazine.co.uk